UNDERCOVER

And Other Stories

Dominic O'Sullivan

© Copyright 2014 Dominic O'Sullivan

All rights reserved

This book shall not, by way of trade or otherwise, be lent, re-sold, hired out, or otherwise circulated without the prior consent of the copyright holder or the publisher in any form of binding or cover other than that in which it is published and without a similar condition including this condition being imposed on the subsequent purchaser. The use of its contents in any other media is also subject to the same conditions.

ISBN 978-1-910176-30-6

MMXIV

Published by
ShieldCrest
Aylesbury, Buckinghamshire, HP22 5RR
England
www.shieldcrest.co.uk

Also by Dominic O'Sullivan

Icarus in Reverse and Other Stories

Shippea Hill (Collected Poems)

To Peter and Mary

With special thanks to Lee Matheson

About the Author

Dominic O'Sullivan was born in North London and grew up in Muswell Hill. He has, however, spent much of his time in East Anglia. He studied German at the University of East Anglia under the guidance of his tutor Dr W.G.'Max' Sebald.

In 2009 he published his first collection of short stories 'Swifts' of which the title story was performed as a play in the Chocolate Factory, North London.

In 2013 he published a second collection of short stories 'Icarus in Reverse' of which 'New Wave' and 'A Dash of Soda' were performed at the ADC Theatre in Cambridge in May 2013 and 'Birdsong' the following year in May 2014 as part of a season of monologues and duologues.

In the same year his plays 'Stray Paths' and 'Forbidden Fruit' were also performed as part of the First Stage season of new writing.

In this collection the title story 'Undercover' was also performed at the ADC Theatre in May 2014.

Contents

Undercover 1

The Dinner Guest 5

Looking East 14

Moving On 19

A Cloistered Existence 27

Breathing Space 36

Listening for George 54

Naturally 65

The Uninvited 75

Without Doubt 84

The Age of Enlightenment 90

Late Call 97

Out of Sight 102

Voices in the Dark 111

The Pump 114

After Class 118

The Ladies' Quarters 126

Afternoon Tea 137

Rookery Nook 144

Blazing a Trail 153

A Drop of Sun Tan Oil 157

Wind	169
The Outside Element	174
Pennies	186
Silent Plunder	191
The Moment	198
Switzerland	208

Undercover

The room is still and silent. It is the room of a dream, a dream that comes back and back to haunt me, with increasing regularity. Into this room, slowly, comes a hand, a pair of hands, milky-white and soft. Gentle hands - but these hands, I'm bound to tell you, are going to cause a revolution.

I look at Rory, spooning Cornflakes - milk flying off the swiftly raised kitchen implement. It catches the sun for a second, but it's not as good as the knife, which sends sparkles round the breakfast table.

He gets up quickly, wiping his mouth, and says simply, "I gotta go." The clock confirms this; college time. The West Greenstead and Ditchling College time. I see him in the yard, opening the shed where his bicycle is kept, and as his trousers press tightly against him as he mounts the saddle; I think how beautiful he is. I would like to be that saddle now - I am deeply envious of it, holding him, supporting him, as I sway beneath him. His mop of dark hair and long arms crouch over the handlebars, and the bicycle is out of sight, on its way to the college catering department, leaving me alone in the house now.

I put the breakfast dishes in the bowl; his dishes, mine, merged together in an aquatic sprawl - my dishes lying on top of him.

He will be cycling over the level crossing, feeling the divots as the bike thuds down hard on them and, with a glance to the left - I'm sure it will be the left - he looks up the empty railway line. It had better be empty, there have been too many accidents of late….. and talking of accidents……

Once the dishes are drying neatly on the rack I climb upstairs, softly, as I always do, in case anyone is about. The door to Rory's room is closed, so I turn the handle gently and slip inside. Immediately I'm inside the room there is a smell of Rory - a good smell, a distinctive smell. The room is in half-light, as if awaiting the presence of a lover; curtains half-drawn, the bed unmade. The window is open, leaving some of Rory to seep into the garden.

There is a pair of football shorts and a red tee-shirt on a chair, but he hasn't worn these for a few weeks now as the season ended. Instead there are the gruff spikes of cricket boots, but alas the whites in which he looks so cute - dark on white - are nowhere to be seen. Neatly stowed away in a cupboard, in readiness for the first game.

I can see him running in, dark hair flopping, and with this pleasing image, I take off my shoes and socks, all my clothes, thrown quickly into a little bundle, and dive into his bed.

There is Rory on the sheets and on the pillow. The unmade bed is cool and welcoming. It's like jumping into foreign waters, both different and familiar, as I splay around in delight in my new domain.

Suddenly the garden gate goes click, and for a moment I freeze in panic; the rasping sound of the letterbox and the clattering of falling mail announces the postman at the door. I slink back under the covers and then, to add to my panic, the bell rings. What am I going to do? What does he want? There's a long silence and I tiptoe softly to the window, cool in my new nakedness, to peep through the curtain chink.

The postman's in a strange position, stooping or something - but then who am I to talk? Look where I am, an interloper in another's bedroom. I get dressed, rumbled in part by the unsuspecting postman, (or is he?), who leaves the gate open and disappears down the lane.

I click the door gently to, goodbyes now to the realm of Rory, who must be at college, bending to lock his bike in the ramshackle bicycle shed.

I once suggested that we got a tandem, but he rejected it out of hand, called me a wimp and said it would be him doing all the cycling. Much better perhaps to ride two on one, I thought afterwards in consolation.

So this is my morning routine to slide into...

I'm packing my bag. It's not too late, and if I run, I can catch the bus that goes from round the corner. It's time for me to go to college, only no cakes and pastry or waiting on simulated customers, just books and poems and a slimline volume of Voltaire's letters. French at 3.

I wonder what time it was in the room, the room I told you about, when she came in - for it must have been a she. The moment that changed all our destinies, singly and as constellations, and sent me ricocheting off in another quite different direction.

How can you know? I hear you say, for you wouldn't be the first. This is some kind of fantasy just like... But on both counts I'd beg to differ. And as for the second, it's a reality too, for I stole into a bed, a real bed before the postman came to interrupt everything.

The reason I came to know is because I eavesdropped. Two aunts talking... A private conversation in the summer house and, well I'd returned home early from college unannounced. Mr. Touquet was ill, so Voltaire had the afternoon off, being left to languish in my locker and according me a double period of freedom. I'd planned to surprise them and sneak right up on them, but something made me stop and I hovered for a moment behind the hedge.

"Gemma thinks so more and more," I could hear Jane say. Her listener gave a mild affirmative grunt. "She thinks there was a mix up, a muddle and somehow they got swapped round."

"But what about the labels, surely? They always have."

"Well...." A silence. The grass was tickling my shoes.

"It may have been done deliberately," a voice said after a while. "After all, she could never be sure."

"But who..?"

The sentence vanished in mid-air as I ran back in shock towards the house. I'd heard enough.

And then I knew. Well perhaps I'd always known. Looking at photographs seemed to convince me all the more.

So that was when I started to look at him closely, to go into his room. For if he wasn't my brother, then it wasn't the same and it wasn't wrong to look at him; to watch him after a shower, drying himself off. He always left his bedroom door ajar, as if he were proud or wanted to be discovered - proud of his prowess, which in turn hypnotised and fascinated me. Only when he leaves for college, when he leaves the house, does he shut his room - as you already know.

And then a little voice says, "But he is your brother, you've grown up with him."

And another voice says, "But it's not the same, the same blood, so you can. Same blood!

I like that voice, and as I listen to it, I close my eyes, feeling those invisible hands lifting me up, taking off the labels, lifting me......changing me forever.

The Dinner Guest

"Please come in, Jane," said Emily.

"Thank you."

Jane negotiated the wide marble step and entered the spacious hall.

"I thought we'd eat al fresco," Emily said. "What with the weather being so good."

"Sounds good to me," Jane replied.

Emily took her coat and ushered her into the living room.

"I thought a Pimm's beforehand. I know you British like to drink."

"Welsh, actually," corrected Jane.

"Pardon me?"

"Welsh."

"What is that?" Emily asked. "Is that a drink you'd prefer? I've not heard…"

"It's a nationality," said Jane.

Emily laughed. "Of course it is. Yes. There's me concentrating on the food and drink. So sorry. You'll have my undivided attention in a minute."

"I look forward."

Emily made her excuses and went off to the kitchen to slice the cucumber. Jane wondered if there was a maid to do such things. It was that kind of house. But no, Emily returned having duly chopped the cucumber and oranges and handed her guest the promised drink.

"We moved here in the fall. We still have the house in town, but it's Larry's intention to spend more time here."

"It's a beautiful house," said Jane. "And a beautiful view."

Beyond the sitting room window, the trees glinted in the autumn sun. Some of the leaves were turning bright red and gold.

"Fall here is just out of this world."

"I can believe it," Jane said, whose own garden boasted no more than an orange pyracantha and a honeysuckle.

"Do you have a garden?" Emily asked, as if reading her thoughts.

"Yes. It's quite compact. There's a winter honeysuckle and pyracantha. She could picture them vividly; the first with its lime-shaped leaves and scent of oranges. It was a welcome sight in the dark, damp winter months.

"What was that last one?"

"A pyracantha."

"Isn't that someone who sets fire to buildings?"

"Maniac," said Jane. "Pyromaniac."

"Oh yes," Emily laughed. "I'm mixing it up."

"Like your drinks," thought Jane.

"And the other one's a honeysuckle?"

"Yes."

"But it comes out in winter."

"That's right.

"That must be all this climate change they talk about. Though, I think it's greatly exaggerated."

"It's meant to come out in the winter," replied Jane. "I like it very much."

"I'm sure you do." Emily drained the rest of her Pimm's. "And are you enjoying your vacation?"

"I am," said Jane. "I come mainly to see family. You know, seeing as they've moved here."

"They made a wise choice," Emily said. "It's so much better for children here. All this space. In Britain you seem to have so many cities stuck together."

"In the north, certainly," Jane admitted. "But there's some lovely countryside, too. There are the moors."

"Too crowded," Emily said. "I was there once. Too many kinds of people. I was visiting an aunt two years ago. Somewhere by the sea. They made that film with Meryl Streep there."

"Out of Africa," said Jane, not thinking.

Emily gave her a bemused look, her eyes bulging further in their sockets than the Murder She Said lady.

"I don't think so," replied Emily.

"Lyme Regis."

"That's the place. Though it didn't sound English to me. You see, they had the 'Lime' with a 'y', you know. It must be because it's so near to France."

"You've travelled around, then?"

"Not as much as we wanted. Aunt was reluctant to go many places. She said it was her arthritis. I'm not surprised with all that rain."

They ate on the terrace; a white scrubbed table, two iron chairs. Emily brought out the plates; pale fish hiding under a lemon sauce.

"Help yourself to salad."

"Thank you."

Jane tried to delay her consumption of the meal for as long as possible. Two spoonfuls and it would have been gone while Emily, with her bird-like appetite, pecked away delicately and thoughtfully.

"It's such a lovely setting," Jane remarked, looking at the trees that sloped down into the valley. "So much space."

"No neighbours," Emily said. "It's real peaceful. I suppose you're all on top of each other where you are."

"In a manner of speaking," Jane replied. "Though it's nice to have neighbours sometimes."

"Larry likes to be self-sufficient. 'Rely on your own resources,' that's what he always says."

"Will he be coming back? Will I see him?" Jane asked.

"Unlikely," Emily said. "He likes me to entertain my single girlfriends when he's not here."

"Oh," said Jane.

"In fact, he's probably at his club. He usually is at this time."

"That's the one in the brochure in the living room, with all the fountains?"

Emily nodded.

"And that includes widows, I suppose?"

"Excuse me?"

"Single people."

Emily laughed, slightly uneasily, perhaps realising, in her devotion to Larry, she had said the wrong thing.

"Have you ever been to the club yourself?"

Emily shook her head.

"Is it men only?"

"No, no," said Emily. "It's an enlightened establishment, I guess. Women are allowed in but I don't think he'd like me cluttering up the place. The men withdraw after dinner and smoke those nasty, smelly cigars. Truly awful. When he comes back he smells like the compost heap."

Jane laughed. It was the first humorous thing Emily had said.

"Do you tell him that?"

"I tell him to go take a bath."

"It stinks all over the clothes and on the skin," said Jane.

"I fail to see the attraction," Emily continued.

"Bonding, I suppose."

"Something like that."

It was nearly nine when Jane decided to head back.

"I'll call you a cab," Emily suggested.

"It's okay, Emily. I'm happy to walk."

It was less than a mile to where she was staying.

"Nonsense. It's the least I can do."

"I'm quite happy, really!"

"It's not done, honey. The police'll stop you. They'll think you're a lady of the night."

Jane quite liked Emily's title. "I wouldn't mind being stopped by a policeman," she said. "Do you know them? Are they good looking?"

Emily ignored her. "I'll go call them."

She left her alone in the sitting room while she went to make the call. Jane wandered around for a few moments, looking at the paintings that embellished the walls. There was one of an anaemic nymph languishing in a wood. She had scarcely time to cast her eyes over the third when there was the screech of car tyres outside, followed by heavy footsteps on the gravel path. The taxi had already arrived; she was most impressed.

Suddenly, she heard a door inside the house open and close. A moment or so later, there was the sound of animated voices. It didn't sound like the taxi driver. A man's voice, maybe Larry's, rose distinctly above Emily's.

"Come and see..." she thought she heard her say, but the other speaker was clearly not having it.

"Are you kidding? I've got other things to do," came the reply.

A few minutes later, Emily re-entered the room.

"Taxi's on its way," she said nervously. "Is there anything else you'd like?"

"No, no, I'm fine," Jane replied.

Returning to the living room, her hostess seemed smaller, less confident. It was as if she was no longer in charge here, Jane thought. The one who really ran the show had returned and, by the sound of things, was clearly not going to grant an audience.

"Thank you again," said Jane, waving from inside the cab. "Give my regards to..."

Emily's figure disappeared from view as the cab glided smoothly down the long drive. The cab's mirror revealed lights on now in the upper parts of the house. Larry had achieved his aim. Jane had been truly invisible.

It was a week later on the same day that Jane found herself wandering round the centre of town. She wanted to buy a couple of magazines for the return flight home. She would find everything in Dixie's, she was told. Dixie's famous department store that straddled the main square downtown.

It was after buying the magazines, mainly full of shots of vibrant, autumn landscapes, that she passed the ladies' department. She had not intended to come this way, but nevertheless, she was intrigued to see what was on offer.

The vast store seemed to drift into infinity; endless aisles piled up with dazzling displays of goods. And then suddenly something caught her eye. She looked at it for a minute or two and deliberated. Yes, of course. It would do nicely. Perfect, in fact. She would take it.

"Would you like a bag?" the assistant asked her.

"I think so," Jane replied. "Oh and where can I find lipstick?"

"Second floor. Downstairs."

In the end, she made a total of three purchases and headed back on foot to the villa where she was staying.

Tomorrow was her last full day. Her hosts, Dan and Lois, would be out till about 6 p.m. Was that okay? Was she happy to amuse herself till then? She was. Then they could eat together afterwards.

It was just before midday when Jane put her plan into action. The house was empty. She picked up the phone and dialled the number she had written down. It was where Emily said he worked.

"Oh yes. Could I speak to Larry, please?"

"Is that Mrs. Considine?" the receptionist asked.

"It is." Her first try of the accent seemed to be convincing and it was easy to do Emily's meticulously clipped voice.

"Well, Mrs. Considine, he's at the Alhambra this afternoon."

"Silly me," said Jane, alias Emily. "The dining club. I clean forgot. No, there's no message. I'll talk to him later."

Out in the street, the first person she asked didn't seem to know the Alhambra but the second was more helpful.

"It's opposite Fontana Park, behind Dixie's. You can't miss it."

Fontana. Of course. The fountains. And Dixie's.

"Thank you," she drawled.

"You're not from round here, lady?"

"No. Not exactly," replied Jane.

It was easy to sidle into the loo at the entrance lobby of the Alhambra, and it was there that she undid her bag. Taking out the newly-purchased lipstick, she applied it liberally, marvelling at its strident colour. Then she rubbed a little powder onto her face, which made the lipstick stand out even more. Finally, to crown it all, she reached into the bag and lifted out the luxuriant blonde wig from Dixie's. On leaving the washroom, she passed by the doorman who reciprocated her smile.

"Can I help you, ma'am?"

"I don't think so," she replied.

"You've come to see someone?"

"Yes."

"May I enquire?"

"Larry. Mr. Larry Considine. My cousin."

"He's expecting you?" The doorman drew himself up slightly.

"Oh yes," she said and smiled.

They were still eating dessert when Jane entered the dining lounge, known as the Long Room. About twenty men in all were seated round a huge, circular table in animated discussion. There was a gradual lull as they became aware of another presence in the room.

"Larry!" Jane cooed, breathing in the smell of raspberry pavlova. There had been a photo of him at the house, but the nervous and puzzled reaction was enough to identify her victim. She perched on the end of the table and crossed her legs.

"I know you always said not to come here but it's just, well, you're getting a little behind…" She paused momentarily for effect. "With your bill."

There was a gasp from someone round the table.

Larry was immediately on his feet. "Do I *know* you?"

He sounded just as she imagined.

"Come now, let's not be coy, Larry. I'm sure your secrets are safe amongst all your friends. I mean, it's not as if Emily ever comes here."

She thought she heard a pronounced gulp.

"It's just the last two times you've come to see me without your wallet and… well, it's getting to be a little awkward. You know, the overheads."

There was a deathly hush.

"But it's okay. No harm done. I'm here now, aren't I? We can settle it here, honey."

Larry seemed to stagger backwards.

"I…I think there must be some mistake. I've… I've …"

"No, Larry. No mistake. Only the last two visits. You know, when Emily was at those poetry readings…."

There were several gasps from the older diners.

"Personally, I've never understood Walt Whitman."

Larry was turning to those seated round him. They looked more like the frosted members of a jury.

"I've never met this woman before," he insisted. You have to believe me."

Jane was standing closer to him now; a smile still decorated her lips.

"I think you've got me confused with someone else. It's a mistake. Call security!" he barked.

But security was already there. They escorted Jane, wobbling somewhat precariously on her high heels, towards the entrance. Larry was only a few steps behind, his protestations now peppered with expletives. If anything they escorted him slightly more firmly. As he was dragged out into the lobby, he was still vehemently protesting his innocence.

"I'm well aware of club rules. Yes, of course I am. But you've got to believe me. I never *met* this woman! Never clapped eyes on her till now!"

Looking East

I should have smelt a rat from the start. Should have read the signs. In general, there was something not quite right, especially when he said "only joking". It was probably to put my mind at ease. But the damage had been done and I've only myself to blame.

Musicians are a cliquey lot and sometimes the whole thing is stultifying. There's a lack of imagination and common sense.

I went to a play once. My flat-mate was in it. Acting school, you understand, but they gave it some welly. In actual fact, I've been to better things there than on the big stage. It's more intimate and apart from some flat intonation, I can pick up the voices better. Get a real feel of it. Anyway, in the bar afterwards, they started ripping each other (well, the absentees rather) to shreds. It came as a disappointment because I experienced that high too. The high of performance. And now the magic was being dismantled clumsily, haphazardly, and I was regretting that glass of oddly warm Europiss.

Of course, there were compliments to those present; lots of kissing, hyperboles, over the top stuff, and I did manage a few words myself. I said it was really, really good. And Jason, who sat next to me, said "Do you think so? You don't think Amanda was speaking too slowly?" And I said no, because I was listening carefully to her voice. It was rich and creamy but with a sad, poignant edge. I could picture her doing Shakespeare – well, almost anything, but alas, Amanda, the absentee, was having some of the gloss chiselled off her.

Jason walked me home and I said how I'd like to meet someone. There must be plenty of scope at the Academy, he said. But I wanted to meet someone, non-musician, not theatre – someone with a foot in the real world, was probably what I said, or he said. Perhaps it was me then, because afterwards he laughed and said, bit of rough, perhaps, barrow boy. And he's right because when I listen to Cockney spoken by some guys, it sounds quite beautiful, and Darren from Bow, who was with me at college, sounded just like that. When I was able to see, he was quite handsome and his brother was a real stunner. But somehow we just didn't gel. You know how it is. Conversation had those empty spaces, those lonelinesses, as if we were groping in the mist. There was no spark of fire that you could warm your hands to, unlike Adam.

So I tried those boxes, apprehensive at first, but it was easy to do. You do an ad and then nothing happens and then three weeks afterwards, your phone never stops ringing. I was worried that something indiscreet might turn up on the answering machine, so I used to take the calls – usually when friends were round for dinner. They used to smile because they knew what I was up to, and after a conversation, I used to come back beetroot red, apparently.

So I changed it to where I could collect the messages – a vast improvement – and arranged to meet. Much better that.

The first was Ron from West Ham. He seemed all right, but when we met in the café, all he did was talk about trains. Could combine it with our meeting. Did I want to come, do a bit of train spotting. I said it was hardly ideal, as I'd have to rely on him as a witness to these momentous moments. Class 42, Elephant Jumbo or whatever. Ron lacked a sense of irony. Shame they don't sell them in Woolworths. Well, I'd hardly make it up, he moaned, seeing as you… well, it would spoil it all, wouldn't it? I declined politely and left, saying that I liked trains when I was in them and they were preferably moving.

Then there was Alfie from Alperton, a place I'd never heard of. Is it America, I asked, as I could hear a faint, unrecognizable twang? No, West London, he said. And I watch a lot of soaps. No good. I had to draw the line at West London. It's probably almost as bad as south of the river. My mate Mark once said you could drop someone in Bedfont or Kenton or Kingsbury and they wouldn't know which one it was. He may have said Pinner too, but I disagreed on that as I once played in the church and liked it there. It reminded me of an old Soviet joke where Vassily gets roaring drunk one night and comes back to his apartment. Turns the key in the lock and there's this woman in his bed who screams. What are you doing in my apartment, he roars. Your apartment! It's mine, you potato-head! After much wrangling he says, this is flat 14? Yes. Block 10? Yes. Ulitsa Lenina? (That's street, by the way) Yes. Just off Peace Square? Again she nods. Yes. Leningrad? Leningrad! This is Moscow, you buffoon! Shit, he says, or words to that effect.

Anyway, it was no good with Alfie from Alperton. I sensed he wanted to take care of me, stifle me, smother me. Not in the literal sense, you understand. But you have to do some things yourself, don't you? And if I walk into the broom cupboard by mistake, so what? Four eyes Fred often goes into the Ladies by accident – or that's his story. And I must admit I had problems with ducks and drakes once at the Anchor and Hope. I kept insisting that ducks sounded the right one. It's all those relatives from Nottingham! That pub was once called the Blue Anchor but changed its name for practical reasons.

So finally I came up with Joe from Barking, the place where all the sewage goes. And I don't know what it was but he had something familiar in his voice, so I said come over here. Ron had given me an aversion to railway stations, and as I'd fallen over the dog a week before, my ankle was still sore.

On that particular day, Janice, my neighbour upstairs, was going to a soufflé conference — so it seemed quite apposite.

Yes, I know what you're going to say. I shouldn't have. Milk poured from the carton always ends up halfway across the table and there's no use whingeing. We got on all right. He was dark, brown eyes, as he described himself. Had an Italian uncle – didn't speak it, though. And that voice! Pure Darren, but with more roguishness – abrasive, wide-boy type. And he was considerate. Instinctively knew about certain "fings". Not like those dozy musicians. And yet he only said "fing" once, and I wondered if the accent was exaggerated like the name and the Italian uncle.

It was when we were on the sofa, separated from my underpants, when he suddenly said, what's this worth? My staccato Queen Mary "pardon" disarmed him, so he relaxed his hand for a moment, let out an embarrassed guffaw and squeaked, only joking. And I relaxed my hand too and it took me a few moments before I could get rhythm and composure again.

Of course, I got a right bollocking when I told my mate Lenny that the credit cards had gone. What did you expect, you pineapple! There's a pecking order of "fruit abuse" and pineapple's near the top. Well, he said he was going to the bathroom, I said and could…. It's throwing caution to the wind, rebuked Lenny, who felt like a cliché at that moment. You broke all the golden rules. Once a dizzy queen, always a dizzy queen, I replied.

But it was no laughing matter and Lenny was furious. He's right of course. He invariably is. He got me to report it and they sent a young copper round to see me. He held my arm when I tripped over the dog again.

Can you give us a description, sir? Was there more than one of them? Then he stopped immediately, aware of his faux pas. It's all right, I said, However, the part of him that I could best describe to you and that I had more intimate acquaintance of, may be of no help to you. Unless, of course, you've changed your interrogation methods. He thought for a moment and I heard him put his pen and notebook down.

You're right, sir, he said.

I started listening carefully to the voice. He could be no more than 23, 24. Finally, I grabbed the nettle, plucked up courage. What's your name and where do you come from, I asked, sounding oddly like a former TV programme. Vincent....from Goodmayes, he said.

Perfect, I said.

Moving On

"I'm Tina," said Tina.
"Pleased to meet you," said Larry. "Moved in at the weekend, did you?"
She nodded.
"I heard a lot of humping."
Tina Fox blushed slightly.
"Boxes, I mean. Moving. Er, where did you live before?"
"Wardle End," Tina said.
"Ah, very nice," said Larry. "Bit quiet, though, I expect."
"There's no pub," Tina confided. "And it was a bit of a walk to Mile Cross."
"Ah yes. It's good to have a focal point. A place to meet. Some of these villages can be a bit lonely."
"There was a phone box," Tina said. "That was about it."
"Yes, I know," said Larry. "The one on the green."
There was a silence. There wasn't much to say after the invocation of the telephone box.
"Well, I'll leave you to it. The rest of your moving in. Er, if you need anything, we're always here."
"Thanks," said Tina.
"Who was that?" Esme asked when he came back in from the garden.
"Our new neighbour, dear."
"She's rather young."
Larry wondered if that made her ineligible for such a title. "Is she, dear? I hadn't noticed."
"You lying toad, Larry Elmswell!"

"Well, she can't help that. She used to live at Wardle End."

"Did she? Well she must have a bit of cash to live over there."

"Didn't like it apparently. Too quiet."

"Well I hope she's not going to make a noise here."

"I very much doubt it," said Larry defensively. "She seems a nice girl."

Most days after their meeting, Tina could be seen sunbathing in the garden.

"She doesn't seem to do much," Esme remarked. "In the way of work, that is."

"Probably doesn't need to," said Larry. "I mean if she lived at Wardle End."

"It's not good," continued Esme. "A lack of work makes one idle."

"Perhaps she's a teacher," Larry suggested. "Some of them can afford houses. She's probably just enjoying the summer. It's been a while since we had a settled spell of fine weather, so good luck to her!"

The next day Larry brought a bag of potting compost up to the first floor balcony.

"What are you doing?" she asked.

"I thought I'd put these boxes up. You know, a few plants. Bit of colour."

"You've never bothered before."

"Got it off the gardening programme, didn't I?"

Esme gave Larry a bad-tempered glare. At times he would revert to an annoying habit of concluding every statement with a question. It was his covert code for 'bugger off!' She knew better than to continue her line of interrogation. Watching him from the window, she saw him pot up half a dozen red and pink geraniums.

"Looks much better, dunnit?"

Esme nodded. The balcony was uncharacteristically colourful. Normally it played host to a mere watering can and obsolete fly-spray, but now the brightly coloured heads of pelargoniums bobbled up and down in the wind.

"I think I'll take the paper outside," said Larry after he had finished.

What Esme could not know, unless she took up position from Tina's garden, was that the flower boxes hid any balcony spectators from view, so that Larry could gaze into the neighbouring garden and observe Tina's lengthy hours of sunbathing in her skimpy, minimalist bathing costume. The gap between the flower boxes was perfectly positioned so Larry could see out while no one could see in.

His spirits rose at the sight of Tina, the newspaper spread across and covering an almost permanent appreciation. He gave a grateful sigh; so glad the spindly Douglases, who rarely spoke, had vacated their property in favour of Tina.

"You don't normally like sitting out," Esme commented.

"Well, with the balcony so nice, I thought I might as well. Besides, I'm a gentleman of leisure now. It's a whole new world."

And so it was. Larry would hear the welcome sounds mid-morning of Tina opening out the portable table on which she would place a book, a jug of iced water and a glass with a slice of lemon. Sometimes she would bring out a small dish of olives.

"I had a holiday in Spain," she confided one day to Larry. "I couldn't get enough of it."

"Oh!"

"Such gorgeous food, I mean."

"I'm sure," replied Larry, who only recently was under the impression that paella was a type of coffee liqueur.

"Tia Maria," said Tina. "Auntie Mary. I'll make you one if you like."

"So it's not paella?" Larry inquired.

"No," said Tina. "It's a Catalan dish."

"So it's not Spanish, then?"

"No." Tina thought for a moment. "I think it is."

Larry blamed Esme for their lack of travelling. Ever since she had puked on the ferry to Dieppe and subsequently been stung by a weaver fish, she had been loath to leave the country.

"I'm not made for travelling, love," she had said. "I'm just no good at it."

And that had been it. Finished. The world had ended near the Normandy coast.

The late autumn and winter proved a gloomy time for Larry. Tina's garden lay deserted in the onset of wind and rain. He cast a vigilant eye through the bedroom window for any signs of activity but there was nothing. It was as if the whole neighbourhood had plummeted into hibernation. Occasionally, he tended to the soil-filled boxes on the balcony and thought with anticipation of the summer ahead. Things would be better then. Definitely. He would get out his shorts and sit once again in permanent contentment in his usual chair.

The days grew shorter then longer. February with its dreary mist gave way to the winds of March and at the appointed time they duly put the clocks forward to rob themselves of an hour of superfluous sleep. As if on a timer, the sudden warmer days of April produced a new Tina out in the garden. The green bikini now alternated with a bright red one.

"Hello," said Larry when he was down at ground level one morning. "I haven't seen you for a while."

Tina flashed a smile from impeccably white teeth. "Nor me you, stranger."

"Been anywhere?" he asked.

"Oh this and that," she replied, which he felt revealed a tantalisingly enigmatic nothing for an answer.

"It's lovely and warm, isn't it? Unseasonal."

Larry nodded and quickly nipped up to his strategic position on the balcony. He had to shift one obdurate flower box slightly to the right as Tina's chair had moved to a different angle. He leaned back in his seat and gazed in contentment as Tina idly flipped through her magazine, crossing and uncrossing her legs in the early afternoon sun.

"Yes, it is," he thought. "Lovely, warm, a little hot even."

It was when he brought back Esme's books back two days later from the library that she broke the news.

"They've moved next door."

Larry was mortified. How could such a thing have happened?

"But she's only been there a few months!"

"I don't mean that topless floozy. I said *they*. The Hamiltons."

The relief was palpable. It swept over Larry as a great wave of comfort. But when had Tina been topless?

"They've bought a bungalow in Weston-super-Mare."

Larry wasn't sure if Esme's comment implied some kind of judgement.

"They were nice and quiet, though."

"He was a retired librarian. What do you expect? All those years of training. I don't know who we shall get now."

"I'm sure they'll be nice, dear. After all, we don't hear a peep out of Tina."

"It's early days," said Esme, guardedly. "We can only wait and see."

The next two months reigned calm and peaceful. Larry retired to the balcony after lunch, where, from his carefully positioned seat, the radiant Tina was slowly turning from peachy apricot to olive brown.

"Still nobody next door," said Esme. "Fancy buying a house and not living in it."

"Fancy," said Larry, gazing avidly at the recumbent Tina.

"Some people must have lots of money!"

"Another refugee from Wardle End, perhaps?"

Esme gave a cold, disgruntled stare.

It was on the Friday morning that she heard the crash. It sounded like the shattering of glass.

"Larry!" Esme called, but remembered that he'd gone into town to buy a new pair of glasses.

An assembly of animated people, a father, mother and five boys were outside in next door's garden.

"Oh, my word! What's happened?"

Curiosity took her quickly outside.

"Good day, lady!" the man called across. "If you are hearing a big noise, it is because I put prick through a window."

"Brick," the elder boy corrected him. Then to Esme, "He forgot the keys."

"Well," said Esme. "I did hear a crash. It was quite loud."

"I always forget keys," he said. "Welcome to my family! This, Conchita…"

The abundantly dressed lady bowed.

"This boy, very tall, Esteban."

"Pleased," began Esme.

"Then, this Carlos, Javier, Julio and Mario."

They each nodded in turn.

"Buenos dias!" smiled Conchi.

"Conchi is no speaking English but is very good in the kitchen."

"Are you from France?" Esme asked.

The man, who had forgotten to introduce himself, looked incredulous.

"No! From Espain, of course!"

"I see," said Esme, who still had painful memories of Dieppe. "How lovely."

"You live alone?"

"No. My husband's at the shops. He's getting a new pair of glasses."

"You drink a lot?" he asked.

Esme thought this was rather personal, but then realised the mistake. "Spectacles," she said, and mimed a pair of glasses with her fingers.

"Ah, spectaculos," he laughed. "Good. See you later. We go in."

There was the sound of feet scrunching warily on broken glass and for a moment Esme wondered if they really were breaking in. Perhaps it was a highly organised raid. But then burglars didn't stop and chat, did they, let alone introduce themselves? And they had all been so pleasant, hadn't they? Such nice looking boys, too!

A week passed and the noisy neighbours were truly settled in.

"You haven't complained about the racket," said Larry. "What's wrong?"

"I think we should give them time to get acclimatised," Esme said. "They seem very nice, although Mrs. Conchi doesn't speak any English. I suppose it's good to have a family next door. They're really quite well-behaved."

There were a couple of manic screams from the adjoining garden. Larry gave Esme a brief look.

"If you say so, dear."

Fifteen minutes later, the doorbell rang. Through the glass in the front door she could see a tall, swarthy figure clutching something. Esme opened the door to meet the apparition. A smiling bronzed boy was standing in front of her. He handed her a vast china bowl.

"It's for you," Esteban said. "It's a paella."

"Pie yellow?" said Esme, trying to copy the elusive pronunciation. "Well, that's very kind of you, Juan."

"Juan, no. Is the old man. I am Esteban."

"Of course," she said. "How silly! Forgive me. It takes me a while to learn all your names."

He gave another broad grin, revealing brilliant white teeth. He must have been playing basketball, she thought, looking down at his shorts. Being so tall it must be a matter of just dropping the ball into the net. Cheating, really.

"I've got something for you," she announced suddenly. "Just a second."

In the pantry nestled an impressive array of homemade jams.

"Loganberry," she announced, passing a jar to Esteban.

He took it as if she were handing him a precious vase.

"It's very kind," he said. "Thanks."

"Adios," Esme said.

"Adios to you."

Depositing the paella on the kitchen top, she ran quickly upstairs.

If Larry sits a little uneasily now on the balcony mid-afternoon, it's because his post-lunch vigil is no longer solitary, no longer alone. Esme has taken to having a siesta between four and five o'clock, which is, coincidentally, also the time when Esteban and two of his brothers take part in their daily basketball practice.

And if Larry were a little more observant, he would notice, too, that Esme has moved a flower box further along the balcony. She's placed it just slightly to her left so that, from her position of idleness and immobility, she enjoys one glorious, unparalleled and unimpeded view.

A Cloistered Existence

I concede there is a part of it that is vanity, a wanting to see how others fare when charged with the great undertaking, make comparisons, but above all, I suppose, lies the element of curiosity of how would things be? How to cope with the passing of time?

For my desired passage I had to see Sister Andalusia, as she is called. Her geographical title takes us away from the prejudices that one might associate with traditional names. For example, in my time both above and below I have had problems with Henriettas. I don't know why it should be but perhaps there is something in the artificiality of the name, the lack of originality, the plucking from Adam's rib, as it were. Henriettas have invariably been stout, well fed and bred, and coming from the upper echelons, of course, have a predilection for horses. They have been robust, yet unyielding, in appearance tousle-haired with a hint of auburn. It is a name sometimes to set alarm bells ringing.

So I approached the happily neutral Andalusia. She was sitting on a rock, strumming a harp. It is the kind of thing you do up here during the day and serves to emphasise an inherent air of piety, which is so appropriate.

I whispered my request as I was told to do.

"Don't say it too loud," Gabriel advised. "Otherwise they'll all want to..."

A lizard was basking in the sun on a stone, its smooth tongue flickering into the air. It was as if it were tasting and testing it. On hearing my sotto voce murmur, it peered intently then slid underneath a rock. I moved towards Andalusia where the breeze helped to disguise our words. You never know who's listening here; passers-by, insects, lizards even.

"I would like to make a journey," I requested. "A special one. A return. Just for the day. To see how everything is faring. You know, since..."

Andalusia gazed at me for a while. Her clear, blue eyes seemed to be calculating something.

"The Time Tunnel is open just once a week," she informed me. "Ever since the 'incident' we have been having to carry out necessary repair work."

Incident? It reminded me of the jellied eel trader who, despite all odds, had recently joined us. He had complained about something called the 'Northern Line', a transport medium that passed through the City of London.

"But *would* it be possible, then?" I asked.

Andalusia smiled uneasily, patted my hand and said she would let me know in due course.

Due course! Those evasive, non-committal words! I thanked the good lady and said I would look forward to her prompt reply.

"You're soundin' like a businessman, mate," commented the jellied-eel man when I mentioned my interview with her.

Naturally, I avoided the specific reason, the object of my request, as I was instructed. But some while later – weeks you might like to call it, for here, time seems to slowly drift like the mist shrouding a great tree-fringed lake, or as a lazy sea fret which clings stubbornly to coasts – I received a reply in the affirmative.

"It is all prepared," says the lady. "Bring a hat."

A hat?

"The draught is indeed terrible. Some say it is like the wind from a cow's backside."

I gazed at Andalusia in astonishment. It did not go with her image of studious lyre playing whilst ensconced on a melancholy outcrop.

"Gracious lady," I murmured.

Two sunlit days later, I was standing before the great stone that heralds the approach to the cavern. Andalusia slid back the bolt of the heavy oak door. I could already feel the breeze, the sensation of air, which she so inelegantly blamed on a bovine's orifice.

"Keep your hat on at all times! When you arrive, leave it hidden under a bush. It is your passport for return!"

"Should I not keep it with me?" I asked.

Andalusia was adamant. "It must not fall into undeserving, unsolicited or unauthorised hands."

She was abundant in her adjectives. "I shall do as you suggest, my lady."

I kissed her long beautiful hands, marvelled at the wisps of hair blowing around her neck. It seemed a fitting target for my sadly inactive lips. I think she may have read my thoughts, for she blushed in no small degree and was a shade hasty in accompanying me towards the tunnel.

"Hang onto your hat, luvvie!"

A voice. Was it Andalusia's? It had the twang from the area near Hartlepool where we used to serve as apprentices.

I stepped into the darkness, felt the wind, the sensation of being sucked into the void...

I was by a river. A breeze was blowing and instinctively I reached for my hat. Then I remembered the specific instructions and sought to secrete it underneath a bush.

The sun was bright, the waters glinted. Small animals, sheep perhaps, munched contentedly on the lush mounds of grass. Their cries sounded differently from what I remembered but I attributed this to the passing of time. The river was a calm and hospitable companion. I followed its gently flowing water, accompanied its unhurried passage towards the sea and reckoned that in this way I would eventually meet the object of my quest.

After a few miles, there it was, standing on a small undulation, gazing out across the fen. One or two buildings had sprung up around it since, but otherwise it was largely unchanged. I saw the sun sparkle on the newly-installed Lantern Tower – at least it was from my time there, but now with the passing of centuries...

There were strange machines that glided along the roads. I had been warned about them by Desmond the fish-trader. 'Cars', he said. 'Automobiles', although that description was hardly true. In fact, I cared little for them as a particularly foul breath seemed to come out of their rear end, not unlike the lolloping cattle I had been warned of.

I was now at the Cathedral's West Tower, entering under its vast Galilee Porch. As I stepped inside, the building appeared even more enormous. A screen had been taken away from when I was there so that there was an almost unbroken view towards the main altar. As I glanced to the left I noticed a sort of wiggly thing on the wall which eventually tapered into a cross.

"What on earth!" I gasped.

A woman in a blue coat approached me. Desmond had told me of something similar in what he described as a holiday concentration camp on the South Coast.

"Welcome," said the shape. "I am from the Welcome Desk."

An effusive and appreciative bureaucrat, I thought, and one who clearly values her own piece of furniture.

"Good day!" I replied.

She must have noticed my lengthy and alarmed contemplation of the undulating, wiggly line.

"It is the *way* of life," she informed me mysteriously. "Life's pilgrimage."

"Ah," I nodded. I was lost for words.

But wasn't there already a labyrinth at my feet, in keeping with those medieval traditions? Would that not do?

Next I observed a greenish statue with outstretched arms. It was a little on the mendicant side, I thought.

"I notice you ask visitors for contributions," I said.

"We do," she replied.

I wandered down the nave. Thunderous boilers chugged away so that even on this relatively warm day they were still emitting large volumes of heat. I gazed up at the Octagon and noticed the dazzling beams of light. My eyes then fell on the stained glass beneath. It was different; somehow changed. The faces shown were less rotund, less wholesome, more angular now, yet at the same time in appearance, romantic. Then as I turned to the right, I saw as a pair of statues, two emaciated-looking figures. I heard someone call them 'the pipe-cleaner people' as they passed by and laughed. I glanced over again and thought about their observation.

From there I wandered past the entrance to where the choir now sings and saw a coppery gold figure attached to a pillar. Such was its construction that it looked like it was going into orbit so I was momentarily afraid hurried into the sanctuary of the Lady Chapel.

I was little prepared for the sight that lay within! Dazzling sunlight and clear windows with just the odd fragment of stained glass! Where had it gone? But as I looked to the sides it was there that the deepest shock awaited me. All manner of decapitated statues decorated the walls while only monsters, demons and sprites appeared to have been spared. Who had done this, I wondered? What manner of barbarism was this?

A stray monk was drifting around the chapel – one of my descendants, no doubt. He informed me he was on holiday, which I thought was a strange remark, so I questioned him about the headless statues.

"Ah, that'll be the King's followers," he said. "Henry and his son Edward. It was the same with all the glass," he added sadly.

For a moment I could envisage the philistines, the stone-age savages, laying waste to everything before them. Legalised destruction by undiscriminating vandals!

And then, as I glanced up from the scene of destruction, a more hideous spectacle awaited. A large blue statue of a rabble-rousing woman stood above the violated altar. It was roughly hewn, crude and ugly in its execution. I felt it lacked subtlety and grace.

"It was put up for the Millennium," the monk informed me. And then he filled me in on all the historical dates, the Reformation, the various changes in monarchy and religion.

"Of course, the cathedral was closed when the Puritans held sway. It was used as a stable for the Lord Protector's horses."

Protector! A misnomer if ever there was one!

"Impossible!" I said.

So they had passed the year two thousand now and this is what they had done! And from nowhere came the words, spurting out in a volley of indignation.

"I don't mind the Protestants breaking the statues," I said, "for that is what they are called and know perhaps no better. But when they put in junk of their own, then I feel I *should* object!"

Junk? Where had that word come from? Then I remembered I had heard someone using it in connection with food.

The monk, I think, was slightly taken aback by my outburst as we approached the giant statue.

"It looks more like a Viking," I observed. "Or a possible Brunnhilde."

"The choirboys named it Charlie, I believe, after a bra-less gardener on TV." He tittered briefly.

I was highly confused. What was a gardener doing wearing a bra and being called Charlie? And what was TV? I had already seen some of these intimate garments in the windows of trading stations in the High Street and had considered it in poor taste. I sat down for a minute to recuperate, relished the comfort of the cold stone.

"I am glad for your company," I said. "But I am sorry as to what time has bequeathed to the place. Especially in more recent years, I hasten to add."

I had one more place to visit. I said goodbye to my monk companion and he left me to reflect a while. The building began to empty and I could hear the sonorous clanking of a bell somewhere.

I decided to exit from the South Door to view the old cloisters where I had spent many a silent hour but when I stepped out into the fresh air there was nothing to be seen at all. I enquired from someone passing by.

"O, oi don't know, dearie. I int a herd o' iny cloisters."

I was glad that Norfolk and its surrounding vernacular had little changed. I asked of two more people but they scratched and simply shook their heads. Finally, a small woman wearing large glasses and carrying a blue handbag seemed to know.

"I can take you there," she offered. "But we need to hurry! Iceland shuts at half past five!"

I felt this was a non-sequitur and gently smiled. She was taking me beyond the cathedral close, through an alleyway and across a road. I felt this must be the wrong way and said so.

"The cloisters!" I said. "I need to visit the cloisters!"

"That's what so many of our visitors say and I am proud to show you what I am partly responsible for."

Responsible? What was she talking about? We darted down an alley again then across another street and over something oddly called a car park. Entering under an archway I could see a brightly lit trading station on the corner and above the words in bold Gothic letters 'Cloisters Shopping Mall'.

Cloisters? Shopping? This was someone 'having a laugh' as my jellied-eel friend would have said. The cloisters were for refreshing the mind, casting out thoughts, for contemplation. They should not be coupled with perfidious acts of Mammon.

"There we are, dear." She introduced herself as Mavis Gotobed, which I felt was wholly inappropriate for the occasion. And it was certainly not something that warranted advertising! I thanked her for her solicitation and quickly bade her goodbye. I looked on bewilderedly at the contents of the Cloisters. Nearby was Dorothy Perkins and something I believe called Fudge Face. Within was Peacocks and...an apothecary-type place with many packaged herbs.

And I wept at the vulgarity of the Cloisters that had detached themselves from the southern wing of the church, severed from the umbilical cord of righteousness.

"It's what everyone wants," added Councillor Gotobed, ignoring my tears. She had not entirely gone. "Don't worry if you haven't got enough cash, love. I can always lend you some. I'm sure it's for a good cause."

I was nearer to despair than ever. She had taken me for a mendicant friar!

As soon as she had gone, I ran from the reconstructed cloisters and out into the clear illuminating sun. It was not too late to breathe the wholesome evening air. I ran back along the riverbank uncertain as to what had happened to me that afternoon and how I should report it. It would perhaps be used as a pretext to close up the tunnel, forbid further visits.

At least my trip here had only been for a day. I could not have coped with a lengthier spell of time, which would have begun to feel like a period of imprisonment, of banishment almost. For one whose eyes have witnessed sweet Andalusia strumming her gentle lye...

I ran over shorn grass, encountered crater-like cowpats, and as I stumbled I envied the graceful grebes and moorhens sedately bobbing along the Ouse.

"No more curiosity," I called to the attendant river. "It is what did for Felix! I wish to know no more! Never, never go back!"

It was a litany to speed me on to my destination where I could gather up my hat, be sucked back into the Tunnel of Time and be gone. I was never gladder to leave as suddenly, in my mind's eye, I saw the collective horrors of the wiggly line, the orbital figure on a plinth, the irate warrior Brunnhilde, whom they also said was a gardener, and the blasphemous contents of the shopping mall.

On reaching the bush, I scrabbled frantically around. My hat was nowhere to be seen. I pulled away more of the soil. I shouted, I cried, I invoked various heavenly bodies, I began yelling for Andalusia. Without my beret of transport, the Oyster Card to the celestial kingdom, I would be stranded forever in a vulgar, misleading, duplicitous world where names did not correspond to the things they should describe.

I began to take in my animal companions that were grazing quietly by the riverbank. They were steadfastly chomping on the rough grass so that it became an even carpet. At first I thought they were sheep but on closer inspection I could see they were a smaller rather mischievous species of goat. As I gazed over I could see the remains of something familiar in the nearest one's mouth. It gaped back at me.

And then, to my horror, I began to realise...!

Breathing Space

"Come this way, please"

Elena was mildly taken aback. She hadn't expected there to be a receptionist and certainly not one wearing a white smock like at the dentist's.

"Doctor Branik is running a little late. Perhaps you'd like to wait in here."

The receptionist ushered Elena into a small ante-room containing four upright chairs. Even here there was a slightly clinical smell and a pile of magazines, such as you would expect to see in surgeries. She flipped through one of them. They were full of the usual problems. "I can't get an orgasm" and "He doesn't listen to me."

She was browsing through the "He doesn't listen to me" when the receptionist returned.

"This is your first time?" she asked. It made her sound like one of the magazines.

Elena nodded.

"Then perhaps we can just run through this form. It's for clinical records, of course."

Of course.

When she got to the question on height, Elena bridled. "Why do you need to know that?"

The receptionist was obviously skilled in having to justify intrusive or nonsensical questions. "Doctor Branik is a holistic healer," she explained. "He likes to treat the whole patient. Height and weight can be linked to diet and overall health. It's just for the record."

It was sounding more like a State Clinic, but then maybe that's what Doctor Branik was. A refugee from the convoluted and bureaucratic system that conventional medicine delighted in. He was bound to take some of the 'baggage' with him. Here Elena checked herself. For a moment she was sounding more like therapist than patient.

"Family history?" Monika continued. "Parents' occupation?"

"Why is *that* important?"

Monika was clearly used to difficult patients. She was able to trundle out replies like containers on a bottling plant.

"I thought I explained," she said with a touch of acerbity. "We like to build up the whole picture."

We, thought Elena. Who's running the place? The absent doctor or the receptionist?

"You make me sound like a painting."

Monika smiled. "It's just routine, you know. And in the long run it could be useful."

Useful for whom? For the police in one of their raids? And what did she mean by 'the long run'?

She kept these thoughts to herself.

"Bricklayer," said Elena.

"Pardon?"

"He helped to build houses. To build Socialism," she added, with a touch of sarcasm. "And Eva, his second wife, was a doctor's receptionist."

For a moment, Monika wondered if Elena had invented that to score a point perhaps, but no, she looked genuine in her response.

"And the first wife?"

"No idea. I was too young. I can't remember."

"Thank you," said Monika. She closed the folder.

"It's not very cosy in here," Elena remarked, looking round at the waiting room. "It's a bit like a cupboard. Not very relaxing."

"Once we reorganise, it will be better. But for the time being, be a little patient."

"I see," said Elena. That's what she thought she was. At that moment, she heard the sound of an outside door opening and closing. There were hurried footsteps.

"Just one second," said Monika.

"Sure."

She returned to the magazines. From outside came the sound of voices. Monika re-entered the room.

"Doctor Branik will see you now. Follow me, please."

She led Elena into a darkened, oak-panelled room. Seated behind the desk was a tall, slim, white-haired man.

"Good afternoon."

"Good afternoon."

"It's Mrs. Nalepkova, isn't it?"

"The same."

"The same as what? This morning? Ten minutes ago? Yesterday?"

Elena laughed. She hadn't expected such an answer.

"I'm pretty much the same."

"Hmm. Are you sure?"

"Yes. I think so. I'm not in the habit of observing or analysing myself."

"No. Of course not. Very wise. As Kleist pointed out – at least, I think it was him – too much self-awareness, self-consciousness, destroys our natural grace."

"Is he a Pole?"

"No, a German. Though he could have been both, I suppose. Like Guenther Grass."

"You're well-read, then, doctor."

"I like to think so. It's good to read, don't you think?"

"I don't get much time."

"Pity. A book is such a good companion."

"Do I look like I need a good companion?"

"Not necessarily, although I suppose we *all* need a good companion. But isn't that why you're here?"

Had he noticed the engagement ring she was still wearing or was it a calculated guess?

"It may be."

"You seem a little defensive."

"Am I?"

"People are on their first visit. They're a little unsure. It's only natural."

"Are they? Well, at least I'm conforming to a pattern, then."

"Very often."

He sat back in the deep black chair. She had seen one once on an English TV show; contestants being interrogated, answering questions. She glanced up at him. His white hair and beard gave him the appearance of an enlightened prophet.

"And nervous."

"I'm not nervous."

"No. Very likely not. More angry, perhaps. But we're finding our way around, aren't we?"

Was he speaking for them both?

"Yes."

"I sense a separation."

The ring!

"I've only just got here."

"You're playing."

"Playing?"

"Yes, yes. I can see it on your face, my dear. A pain of separation. You still miss him."

"Well...yes." An educated guess. Nothing more. Most visitors were unhappy. No one visited out of happiness.

"Now before we carry on. I think we need to do a little exercise."

"What kind of exercise?"

"A breathing exercise. It's quite important. You see, my dear..."

"It's Elena."

"Yes. Of course, it is. You see, Elena, breathing is an underrated thing. Very underrated. It's sits right under our nose."

"Or in it, perhaps."

He smiled. "Yes, that too. Now what I'd like you to do is to take a deep breath."

Elena inhaled.

"Not yet. Take your time. Slowly. That's it. To the count of four."

"Not five?"

"No, not five. Hold it. Breathe out. Like so. Practice for a few minutes. That's it. In... and... out. In... and out...Focus solely on the breathing. Nothing else. That's it. Keep going. In a few minutes, we will be able to talk better, you'll see."

Elena followed the instructions.

He smiled. "There, you see. Already a difference, don't you think? I can see the tension has dissipated."

"I wasn't tense."

"Just a little. And who wouldn't be? The first meeting with an unknown commodity like myself and, very likely, an oddity to you."

"I don't judge."

"That's good. We do too much of that now."

Elena found herself agreeing.

"Would you like me to tell you about it? About him?"

"How do you know it's a he? It could be a she."

"You said so earlier. Before the breathing." There was a pause. "No, I can see you're not happy."

"How many people come to you because they're happy?"

"Very few, I'm afraid. I wish there were more."

"People don't usually go to the doctor if they're healthy."

"That's because they're schooled in the discipline of corrective not preventive medicine. If more people went to the doctor when they're healthy, then fewer people would come who were unhealthy."

"How do you make that out? There'd be no room."

"There'd be far more room. Do you garden?" he suddenly asked.

"Yes, sometimes. We had one at our summer house."

"If you hoe when there are no weeds, there'll be no weeds. Do you see?"

"I see."

"But we're not here to talk about gardening. What's his name?"

"Daniel."

He placed a pen in the middle of his desk.

"Where did you meet him?"

"In a library."

"A place of erudition. That's good."

She hadn't expected a sense of humour, nor the fact that he seemed to pick up on almost every word. He was obviously a skilled listener. Quite unusual in a man. They normally wanted to talk, to lecture.

"And…?"

"I was looking for a book."

You were in the right place, then." He smiled "Was he working there?"

"No, no. He just seemed to know his way around. I saw him a few times afterwards. I used to go, hoping he'd be there. He was very slim and dark. You don't expect sexiness in a library."

"No?"

"He asked me out and then… Then I moved in. Everything was fine. Once a month he'd go and see his family. They lived in a villa in the country. A beautiful spot, apparently."

"You never went?"

"No. He kept his friends and family in separate boxes. People do sometimes."

"I'm well aware of that. But weren't you both...?"

"We weren't official to them, maybe. I don't know. Then one day, he left as usual to go to work. Only he didn't come back."

"Oh."

"I was frantic, of course. Ringing round the hospitals, police stations, Nothing."

"And you had no idea?"

"No idea of what?"

"Was he planning something? Were there any complications...?"

"You mean another woman? No." There was a brief silence in the darkened room.

"I like your terminology. Complications. Very discreet."

He smiled. "Did you have any idea why he should up and vanish?"

"People do, don't they? They disappear. All the more so in this fragile Federation.

All these wars! So fruitless! A time of madness. The playing of the nationalist card."

He was examining her closely.

"It wouldn't have happened if ..."

"No, no. I quite agree. *He* held the whole flimsy patchwork thing together. That was his skill. Though there were a few mistakes, of course."

"There are always mistakes."

His eyes seemed red, she thought, behind those thick, pebbly glasses.

"Nothing lasts. I wondered perhaps if it was to avoid the army."

He nodded. "It could be. Many people did, though it was often futile. They caught up with them in the end."

"He hated violence of any sort. Now I come to think of it, Daniel was always interested in the Quakers? They're pacifists, apparently."

"Peace and chocolate. That's their philosophy." He seemed almost scornful.

"Pardon?"

"They made a lot of chocolate, some of them. Well, they could hardly make alcohol. At least in England, anyway. Britain, or whatever they want to call it."

"I think it must have been the army."

"And by not telling you, he didn't want to incriminate you?"

"I suppose not."

"So he was thinking of you?"

"Maybe." She reached for a tissue. "It's just so hard. Each day… Every single day. I thought as it went on it would get easier."

"But he was thinking of you. He probably still is. At this moment, even!"

"Then why hasn't he come back? Things are easier now."

"You reckon?"

"Yes. The evil… the evil that lived with us has all gone. Well, nearly. They just need to find…"

"Do you believe in evil?" he asked. "As an entity? That people are born evil?"

"No. I don't know. I don't think so. I think about those working in the camps. The 'cleansing' regime. A daily routine of unspeakable brutality, of horror and atrocity, and then home at the end of the day to family life. Happy families, even. And friends."

"So?"

"Just evil acts. Not evil people. Not born evil. Circumstance. Yes, the combination of circumstance."

"And history?"

"History?"

"Of feeling special. Being chosen?"

"Chosen?" Elena wasn't sure.

"Some would think so. And then of course, long and senseless vendettas. Old scores. Unforgiving memory. *That* can turn people. And naturally each side believes they're right."

"I suppose so." She wanted to return to Daniel not politics. "But why didn't he come back?" she asked. " What happened to him after he left the country?"

"*If* he left the country…"

"You mean? No, that's not possible. Wouldn't they have told me?"

"You're forgetting, aren't you? There were wars on."

"So you think…?"

"It's possible."

"No, it can't be."

"Wouldn't you like to sit awhile? I think we've talked enough for the time being, don't you? Just sit back…"

Elena was too agitated to know what to do.

"We'll talk again soon. I think we've achieved enough for one day. Just take in the room again. Slowly. That's it. Leave in your own time. And remember the breathing. I haven't got anyone till half six."

He got up and left soundlessly. It was like a vision leaving; a ghost departing.

The white coat of the receptionist was a harsh contrast to the muted colours of the room.

"I'd like to make another appointment," she said.

"Same time next week?" said Monika.

She received a phone call on the Tuesday.

"Hello. Elena Nalepkova?"

"Yes."

"This is Monika, Doctor Branik's assistant."

"Oh yes."

"I'm afraid Doctor Branik has to go to a meeting on Thursday."

"Oh."

"Can we schedule it for the following week?"

"What about Friday?"

"Fully booked, I'm afraid."

"Oh."

It was a shock to learn of her un-uniqueness. Talking to Branik had made her feel that she was his only patient, or client, or whatever they called it nowadays. She preferred patient, because that's what patients did – the word originally coming from the French 'patienter' to wait. Waiting for a hopeful outcome, the eventual return…

"Next week, then. There's nothing earlier?"

"I'm afraid not."

"Okay."

"So Thursday 25th. Twelve o'clock?"

A meeting at midday?

"That's fine."

Elena sat down and bit into an apple. Her eagerness to return had taken her by surprise. Another ten days seemed a long time. But then if he was busy, booked and popular, it was probably good to have someone who was so much in demand. There was something about his presence, his appearance that calmed and reassured her. She would have to wait, then; let time drift by.

When Thursday came, it was a damp, grudging sort of day. The traffic meandered sluggishly across town and for a moment she wondered whether she was going to be late. As it was, she arrived with twenty minutes to spare. The receptionist showed her into the waiting room.

"Miss Tomkova."

"Nalepkova."

"Sorry. My mistake."

The waiting room was again empty, only this time slightly warmer than before. A radiator clanked in the corner. Elena wondered how many patients had huddled in the airless room prior to her visit.

She picked up a glossy magazine and flicked listlessly through the pages.

She did not have long to wait. Doctor Branik appeared in the doorway, smiling, and waved her in. He appeared tired to her. A night of broken sleep, perhaps; the strain of listening to a litany of tales and sorrows, the miseries of the world.

"We didn't meet for a while."

"No." Elena sounded almost accusatory.

"I'm sorry about that. We've been busy."

"Of course."

"How have you been? Have you been doing the exercises?"

"Well…"

"Three times a day?"

"Not exactly."

"Twice?"

"Sometimes. Most days once. It's just a question of remembering."

"Ah yes." He sat back. "You know, it's good for the blood pressure, actually."

"I didn't say my blood pressure was high."

"No, you didn't."

"Do you need to take it?"

"I'm not that kind of doctor." His tone was almost disparaging. "It's good for all kinds of things," he persisted.

He peered at her through his small, pebble-like glasses. Even in rebuke, his voice was calm, consoling. The sandals that clung loosely to his feet made her think of sixties' hippies and gurus. Perhaps that's what he was.

"Have you been thinking about Daniel?"

She nodded. Hardly a day went by.

"I think you may be right," she said. "It could have been the army."

"It was *you* who said the army."

"Was it? Oh yes."

There was a long silence. She looked at the rooftops beyond the window.

"Why doesn't he ring me? Get in touch? Things are better now?"

"Are they?"

"Most people seem to think so."

"And you are most people?"

She laughed. "Hardly!"

They fell silent again.

"There's always the possibility..." Branik said.

"Yes?"

"That he doesn't want to come back. That he's scared."

"Of what? Of the authorities? Things have changed, haven't they?"

"Maybe he doesn't know that."

"There's TV, there's radio. He can listen..."

"Oh yes," he smiled. "We had all that."

She suddenly noticed the painting above his head. A bland, almost mythical landscape. In the old days, it would have been a portrait.

"Or..."

He was looking at her closely.

"He doesn't want to..."

Branik waited for her to continue.

"...because he's met someone. I mean, we're free to choose, aren't we? He's got a new life now... I'm just..."

The tears were starting to fall, slowly at first.

He poured out a glass of water from the jug and offered it to her. From the drawer, there was a box of tissues.

"Thank you," Elena said.

"If you want, we can finish," he suggested.

"I think that's maybe best," she said.

Out in the street, the sunlight glared harshly on the glistening pavement. It seemed out of keeping with her mood. Elena decided to walk back through the park to the leafy outer suburbs. The air was cooler, calmer. Time to think. Perhaps she was doing too much of that. Thinking. Daniel himself had said too much thinking was no good. Analysing. Was he thinking of her? Did he ever think of her?

It was on the bus that evening, as she made her way over to her brother's flat, that she decided she would make one last visit to Branik. Three was enough, she thought. Time to move on, as Daniel had always said, and maybe, if she did that, she would find him, by chance even, walking along the street...

Tomas's flat was warm and welcoming.

"We are here to celebrate the life of Gabi."

Looking beyond Tomas's slight frame, she noticed that the fish tank was empty.

Gabi, the porcupine fish had been the subject of many conversations. Occasionally, she blew herself up for visitors, puffing up to nearly twice her size. Like a submerged tennis ball, she bobbed and darted uncertainly through a mesh of brittle weed. The TV was on in the background in the other room. Elena always preferred the radio for company, but given the newly departed fish, she felt she couldn't ask him to turn it off, as she sometimes did.

"I made a goulash," Tomas said. He got most of his recipes from his friend Laszlo, who in turn rang his sister in Budapest.

"Perhaps you should open up a restaurant together."

"Hardly," said Tomas. "No business sense. We'd be giving the food and drink away."

"That's where you need me," she said.

The TV had suddenly become louder, shriller, so that Tomas got up to silence it.

Elena listened. It was one of the hate speeches from the times people referred to as 'the troubles'. It was far worse than that, of course. Neighbour against neighbour; communities set against each other then torn apart. A slow genocide. A cleansing!

"I cannot abide that voice," Tomas said. "Let alone the content. I only hope they find the beast and track him down."

Elena bit the only chilli in the goulash. She ran to the kitchen for water.

"I think I should have used green ones," he said. "Laszlo didn't say."

"You mean he didn't ask," she gasped. It took several minutes to recover. When she kissed him goodnight, her lips were still burning.

"Have you ever been kissed by a dragon?" she asked him.

"Not recently," he said. "Unless you count Auntie Tanya?"

She laughed, despite the chilli.

"Do you have to go back, Elena? There's always the spare room. You don't have to walk across town."

For a moment, Tom, the half-brother reminded her of Daniel in his solicitousness. He was slim and dark like Daniel, too.

"I've got an early start tomorrow," she lied. They kissed again.

The bus was half an hour in coming. Tom's apartment seemed cosy from the ice of the wind-blown street. She thought of going back to him but it was too late now. She had made her choice.

There were two patients in Branik's waiting room when she arrived for what was to be the last appointment. She felt guilty for knowing what *he* didn't. Money had to be a consideration, too. Branik was not cheap. Besides, he must be used to it; patients vanishing into the ether.

She wondered whether the long wait she had to endure was some kind of revenge. The two sombre patients coughed alternately. Losing her status of uniqueness would make it easier to part.

"You look brighter," he observed.

"Do I?" she said. "Maybe it's the breathing."

"That's good."

"I've been going out more. Tomas has been nagging me.

"Tomas?"

"My brother."

"You never mentioned him."

"Half-brother, actually."

"I see. So being half means you mention him less." He sounded glib.

"Of course not."

She could see he was smiling slightly behind those heavy lenses.

"I think he's right."

"He usually is. He's wise beyond his years."

"Not too wise I hope. He could be putting me out of a job."

She looked back at him uneasily. Did he sense anything? Did he suspect something?

"Have you always lived here?" she suddenly asked him.

"In this city, you mean?" He paused. "No. I only have a flat here. I move around. It's the nature of my job. I'm in the country most of the time...when I'm not working."

Elena was surprised. She had never asked him a personal question before. She had always been the sole focus of their conversations. It was a sign, maybe, that she was taking her leave - well, going to - and that at least she would have a grain of information to salvage.

He was talking about a village he had a particular affinity with. A place he could relax; a place where people trusted each other.

There was something he said, something in that voice, which previously had only spoken in short, inquisitorial sentences, that sounded familiar. She found herself thinking back to Tomas's flat, of the room with the TV beyond the fish tank, and then she realised.

"Oh my god!" she cried. She stood up.

"Is something wrong?"

She couldn't bear to look back at him.

"Yes, yes," she said.

She had to get out of there straight away.

He noticed that her hands were shaking.

"Tell me about it," he said quickly.

"I…I've left the oven on at home," she lied, thinking of Tomas's kitchen.

She saw him checking his watch.

"It might burn the place down."

"Well, hardly," he offered, "but if it's a concern."

"I've got elderly neighbours," she replied. "I can't take the risk, the responsibility."

"I could drive you," he said. "I don't usually use the car but I've got a gap…till the next client."

"No, no, it's fine," she said. "If I hurry… "

"I'll see you at our next meeting, then."

He stood up as she saw herself out.

In the street, she was trembling even more. How could she not have noticed? Behind the false inflections, the slightly altered accent, the voice. The same voice! Of course, he was physically unrecognisable; even the most careful scrutiny would probably fail to find a connection.

What to do? She could ring Tomas but he might say that she was imagining it. He would say it was the TV; a coincidence, an association of ideas. She put a hand inside her coat. Her mobile phone hung heavy in her pocket, so quick, so convenient, but she found herself walking the streets briskly in search of a phone box. They were fewer and fewer now; not so easy to find. Better from there, she thought; more private, more enclosed, less exposed.

She got two numbers from the directory. One should suffice.

At the first attempt, she dropped the receiver, but slowly, breathing heavily – even now, breathing made her think of him – she dialled the number. A young man's voice answered, a light, carefree kind of tone.

"It's him," she said eventually, feeling a knot tighten in her throat. "The one they've been looking for. All this time. It's *him*!" And then she said his name.

"You're sure?" the voice said. "You have proof?" There was a pause. "I'll pass you over to my colleague." There was an exchange of words at the other end of the line. Someone had placed their hand over the receiver.

This time the voice was older, calmer, less impressed. "You wish to report something?"

"Yes, yes. It's him! Definitely him! Practising in a clinic near Kostitso."

"I see."

A long pause. The muffled sound of background voices.

The second speaker cleared his throat.

"We know. The authorities already know."

"What! They know?"

"They know. They've known for a while."

"They know and they do nothing! They let a war criminal…!"

Another delay down the line.

"Now is not the right time. A change of climate, maybe. Political circumstances…"

"But… I don't see…"

The gaps in conversation were beginning to make Elena nervous. Looking through the glass of the phone box, she wondered if she was being watched from the other side of the street. She let the receiver dangle while the voice carried on speaking. Closing the door silently, she walked quickly away from the phone box. What if they rang Branik? He would put things together. Make calculations. She had left so abruptly, so alarmingly. An oven on at this time!

Elena turned around. It was no longer safe now to return home; to go back to her flat. She could easily be traced. All the information that was needed lay within Monika's desk.

Walking quickly now, she turned down the ugly boulevard that led to the railway station. If she had had a scarf, she would have wrapped it around her. Yes, she would take the first train; the first one that ran any distance, swiftly out of the country.

She was oblivious to the fact that her shoulder-bag contained no passport. She told herself simply it was time to leave. Leave, go anywhere – anywhere that might take her, lead her back to Daniel.

Dominic O'Sullivan

Listening for George

"May says she's moving," Lisa announced suddenly at breakfast.

Her brother Mark gazed up bleary-eyed in disbelief. "But you said she'd never move."

"Apparently not."

"But I thought you said she said she'd *neve*r move."

"She did. But now she is."

"I can't find the honey," he grumbled.

"It's right in front of you. By that nose of yours."

"Where to, then?"

"Somewhere near the coast."

"That narrows it down to a few thousand places, I suppose. West, south, east?"

"East."

"What's it called?"

"I forget the name. She said it to me twice. Says we must come and visit."

"You don't mean *together*?"

"Do I look that silly? There's no way I'm going away on a break with a spotty, dimwit younger brother."

Mark ignored her as he invariably did; it only made her more annoyed.

"You've got the reactions of a terrapin," she'd said once.

This was nearer the knuckle for Mark, as the one pet that had been granted temporary residence in the living room, in a fairly sizeable tank, had ungratefully escaped and was found spread-eagled upside down in the pantry.

"What was it doing there?"

Lisa's voice was devoid of sympathy. "Looking for food, I expect. The amount you gave it to eat was hardly enough to feed an ant."

"Better to underfeed than overfeed," he'd replied.

"Shame we don't apply that to you!"

"I'm just hungry," he remonstrated.

"No," thought Lisa morosely, who had only recently renounced Bakewell tarts and custard creams. Her brother was aggravatingly slim. "It's not as if you're *any* weight," she replied feebly.

He knew this was sensitive ground for her and let it subside.

"That place?"

She was trying to remember. "It's one of those that's different from how you write it."

"Oh," said Mark.

Three months later, Aunt May was installed in her new home.

"I'm going up to see her next weekend," Lisa announced. "I'm taking Duncan."

"And she thinks *I'm* spotty," Mark muttered to himself. Then to Lisa. "That's nice of her."

"What do you mean? She said to visit."

"I mean, it's not every home that would admit Duncan."

"Admit what?"

"Let him in. He's not for all tastes. Besides, he's terrified of water."

"And how would *you* know that?"

"He hasn't had a wash for weeks."

"Well, you'd know all about that!"

"Meaning what?"

"If you must know, he eats a lot of garlic. It's a predilection."

Mark stopped. This was a word he hadn't heard before. He wasn't sure what it meant, but it stopped the conversation dead, in mid-track, which was just as well, as it was Wednesday and he didn't feel like arguing.

The Friday came and Lisa was in ebullient, cheery mood at breakfast.

"A whole weekend without any interruptions or irritations," she breezed.

Mark reached for the cereal. It was just what he'd been thinking. And with the folks away on some marriage guidance counselling weekend, it couldn't have been better. Late nights in front of the TV, late mornings, copious amounts of all the wrong food. Under the table he rubbed his hands silently in appreciation.

"It had been a brilliant weekend," Lisa announced on Monday morning. Then, as an afterthought. "No college?"

"Not till the afternoon."

"I wish I'd gone to Tech. It seems that classes are cancelled all the time."

"I'm always free on Monday mornings. Shows how much you notice."

"Folks not back?" Lisa asked.

"They rang yesterday evening. The course is quite stimulating, they said, between not being able to stop giggling. They've booked in for another week."

"That's more like it. By the way, she wants you to go up."

"Who does?"

"Aunt May, of course. She wondered if you were going to come up with us, but I pointed out the general irritating nature of your presence and said how it was best for both of us, and that way she'd get two lots of visitors."

"What did she say?"

"She said she could see both our points of view and was looking forward to seeing you. Heaven only knows why!"

"Well that's nice, then," said Mark, by way of concluding the conversation.

"I don't know if she gave you directions," May was saying to Mark on the phone, "but you need to get a slow train from Norwich."

"She didn't."

"And then you can get a bus from the station, only they're not very frequent. I wouldn't get a taxi. They're pretty pricey. If it's low tide, you could walk along the beach to the village."

"How long does it take, auntie?"

"Aren't you forgetting something, Mark?"

Of course. Mark instantly remembered. One of the things May didn't like was to be referred to as auntie.

"I didn't like it when I *was* an auntie and even less now I'm a great-auntie," he recalled her saying.

"About forty minutes," May continued. "Though with those long legs of yours, probably about half an hour. I'll be able to see you from the garden. I'll keep an eye out."

Which was just as well, Mark thought afterwards, since he had no address, and that birdbrain of a sister still couldn't remember the name of the place she'd been to. And she called *him* dim! He would learn the name and, what's more, be able to say it correctly in the way a proper local would. He would find his way around in no time and pass on his superior knowledge quite casually during the breakfast encounters, which was about the only time he saw Lisa these days.

Stepping off the train at the unstaffed railway station, the first thing Mark noticed was the freshness of the air and the smell of the sea. There was an on-shore breeze with flags and bunting draped over the modest pier fluttering wildly as he headed towards the beach.

He couldn't tell if the tide was in or out but as he walked slowly across the sand, he saw that some stretches of beach were less accessible than others. Behind the breakwater was a ridge of pebbles and a wide expanse of water where the sea was coming in. To avoid getting wet, he had to negotiate part of the cliff and immediately noticed how soft the ground was. It was slippery and occasionally sank beneath his feet, but once he'd reached the other side, unbroken sand took him along towards the outskirts of a small village.

"Ma-ark! Ma-ark! Up this way." From the cliff top, a figure waved and pointed to a path that had been carved with small steps up the cliff. Treading on the soft earth, he wondered how safe it was.

"You'll be all right," May called on seeing his hesitation. "It's not too bad. It's much quicker than going round."

On reaching the top, she ran to meet him, giving him a hug and a kiss as she took his bag. "Nice, isn't it?" she said, pointing at the view. "You travel light. Your sister brought half the house with her."

Mark nearly replied with an appropriate comment but stopped himself in time. This weekend would give way to pleasant amnesia. He had no sister he could recall. In fact, he was curiously devoid of any relations, apart from auntie, and he was going to enjoy himself.

"You're in the little room," said May. "You'll like it."

Mark placed his lightweight bag on the bed and opened the lattice window. The sea stretched beyond in a great, brilliant arc whose waves glinted in the afternoon sun. In the distance, he could see a tiny tug plodding towards the horizon. The room felt fresh and invigorating.

"I expect you'd like something to eat," May called out to him.

"Please," he said.

"Good. That sister of yours hardly ate anything when she was here. Almost nothing. Nor did that spotty boy she came with."

"Duncan."

"Was it? I thought she said Dermot. Never said much either. Polite enough, though."

They ate in the garden with the sparkling sea beyond. There was a tree bent over a little-used greenhouse, which showed the direction of the prevailing wind.

"They say it'll be cold in winter," said May. "Bitter winds. It doesn't bother me. I'll be wrapped up with a book inside. Anyway, I like fresh air. Too many of these buildings are overheated. I went to the town hall to pay a bill last week. Only early September and the heating's going full blast."

Mark looked at the unkempt garden around them. "What made you come up here, aunt...?" He stopped himself in time. Didn't fully enunciate the 'A' word.

"I've always loved the sea," May said. "As a kid, you know. And then there was George, of course."

"George?"

"Yes. You never met him, dear."

"You mean my great uncle?"

For once May didn't bridle at the use of title.

"Well, sort of. He was my...partner. We never married. Never got round to it. George didn't like weddings. Let's not go to ours, I said, by way of proposal. To which he laughed and moved in with me."

"And what happened to...?"

"Ah," said May. She fell silent for a while. "He was a sailor was George. I met him in the Vine in Norwich. I can't remember why I was there or what I was doing but I met him one winter's evening in the Vine. He was talking about a place called Yarburg. I'd never heard of it, so, as I'd had two pints of Guinness, I plucked up courage and asked him where it was."

Mark couldn't visualise aunt May ever having to pluck up courage.

"You may not think so, but I was quite shy then. Anyway, to George. 'Well, I travel everywhere in that 'ole boot,' he said.

There were a lot of words I had to get used to. 'And I go to Hamburg and Jotterburg' – don't ask me where that is – 'and Flensburg, so the first thing I see when I come back to Norfolk is Yarmouth, and I call that Yarburg. And Yarburg it is.' I could see the logic in that. So, every day, while I was in Norwich, I went in to the Vine for a pint of Guinness. I put on a few pounds, I can tell you. In the end, we started going out. I don't think they approved in the family as he was that bit older, but he was a lovely, virile man. Oh yes. But one day his ship went down. There was a storm and…"

May was silent again.

"So that's why I moved here, moved to the sea. To be near him. I sit out in the evenings sometimes, when it's nice, just watching, looking at the waves. Silly, isn't it?"

"No, May," said Mark. "It's not. It's…it's the best thing to do."

She squeezed his hand for a moment. Mark wasn't sure if it was for what he said or the welcome omission of 'auntie'. He had instinctively called her May.

"Shame you never met him. Not many people did. He would have liked you."

She got up quickly. "I'll get the pudding," she said. "It's apple pie."

The following evening was unusually mild.

"To think those daft buggers will be keeping the heating on where I go and pay my rates. We'll eat outside then," she announced.

Mark waded through a soup, a casserole and an Eve's pudding.

"There's plenty," May said. "Help yourself to seconds."

He came back with replenished plate.

"It's good to see you've got an appetite. Like my George. He needed his energy, though." She checked herself in time. Mark grinned.

"You don't miss much," she said. "You got a girlfriend?"

"No, not yet," he answered.

"You will have," said May. "Lovely boy like you. They'll be queuing up."

He smiled. "I'll take my time," he said. "Lisa rushes at the first thing on legs."

He then quickly rebuked himself as much for ungenerosity of spirit – away from home he should be slightly more loyal – as for the break in the welcome 'amnesia' that had drifted over the weekend.

"I'll stay out for a bit longer," May said. "It's a nice evening. If you want to watch telly…"

"I've got a book," Mark said. "I'll sit out for a while too."

May was sitting there as he turned the pages, immobile, listening for every sound. The light began to fade. On the horizon, there were shades of crimson and blue.

"Good job we had tea early," she said, breaking the silence. "Yes, we always had it on the early side. Didn't like eating too late."

He nodded.

"There's a torch inside. Don't go straining your eyes."

It was the falling of the book to the ground that woke him. Either that or he thought he'd heard a voice. May was still motionless in her chair. It was dark now and cold.

"Shall we go in?" he suggested, turning to her.

She looked round slowly, as if realising that he was still there, that she did have company after all.

"Yes. You can, love. I'll be in, in a minute."

He fetched a coat from indoors and she wrapped it gratefully round her.

Mark was tucked up in bed when he finally heard the sound of the chairs being put away. There was the crunch of footsteps on gravel and through the open window he could hear the murmuring of the distant tide. It seemed to be getting gradually louder, advancing slowly, marching…

"What time's your train?" she asked him next morning. They had both risen late for breakfast.

"Two fifteen," he replied.

"Then you've got to walk across the beach, unless you get…"

"It's fine. I don't want a taxi."

"Probably just as well. Half of them don't know the way. Would you believe it in a little place like this? I'll do a fry-up. You'll probably be hungry later."

While May was attending to the late breakfast, Mark took a stroll round the garden. It looked different in daylight; smaller somehow. He looked in through the broken panes of glass at the greenhouse. Two geraniums sat in pots; they needed watering. Just beyond the adjoining shed, he noticed that some of the soil had fallen down the cliff. A bush lay halfway down on its side, its roots tilted up towards the drying sun.

"Oh yes," said May, when he mentioned it. "All the gardens used to be bigger round here. It's the soil, you see. Bit of a problem."

She waved him off from the cliff, just as he had arrived. A big cheery wave. The sun was behind her, silhouetting her in the breeze, then she was gone.

When he arrived there, the train was late, so it was not until after three that he finally left the station.

On his return home, he was aware of something different, something strange. It took a few hours for it to dawn on him, but there it was. Most odd. He and Lisa no longer sparked; she was almost civil to him. At first, he wondered if she was sickening for something or whether there was a new boyfriend, but no, at eight o'clock the phone rang as usual and he answered it to the sound of a familiar voice.

"Is she in?" Duncan asked.

"She's in the bathroom."

"Tell her I'll be round in half an hour."

It was not just on the first evening but on the second too. It lasted until the end of the week and beyond. Mark was mystified at the sudden transformation. It went on for weeks, unbroken, like a spell of fine, hot weather. The folks commented on it as well.

"It must be those marriage counselling weekends. Perhaps we should go away more often," they said.

They were a little concerned at the way Mark and Lisa so readily agreed.

It was while they were attending the follow-up course that the phone call came.

"It's Martha Fothergill," the voice said. "May's neighbour. I live at twenty two, three doors along.... It's your aunt...."

It was Lisa who took the call, but when she spoke to Mark it was as if he knew somehow. He was quite calm.

"There was a cliff fall," Lisa said. "Sometime last night. May was outside." It took her a while to say the rest. "There was a high tide..."

Together they took the train, sitting for the most part in silence. It was a bright, sunny day and they walked together along the beach. Lisa did not protest nor even suggest getting a taxi. Pebbles kept getting caught in her shoe.

When they got there the house was silent, the upstairs windows still open.

"She always liked plenty of fresh air," Mark explained.

He walked round the garden while Lisa was inside making a phone call. There was a rose in flower outside the greenhouse; another pane of glass was missing. As he walked round its fragile structure, he gazed at the ground beyond. It seemed to have been scuffed up by something. When he looked more closely, he suddenly realised what it was. Marks from May's chair appeared as swirls across the earth. It had been placed much further forward from where she usually sat; virtually on the edge....

He stared for some while at the tell-tale ruts. Lisa was still talking on the phone.

Reaching inside the shed that was now more precariously placed than ever, he took out the nearest garden implement. It was a rake with some of its teeth missing but it would do. He ran it carefully over the tracks where the chair had been positioned, looking at the lip where the earth had slipped.

Quickly removing any soil from the remaining prongs, he put the rake back unnoticed inside the shed.

As a few spots of rain began to form on the greenhouse, he murmured softly, "Don't worry, May. Everything's under control. You'll see."

Lisa was coming out into the garden now.

"They won't suspect a thing."

Naturally

Mrs. Dehoopney-Mer woke up with a start. In her alarm she had pulled most of the bedclothes up towards her. Untangling herself with some difficulty, she wondered what it was that had woken her. More often than not, it was the fat wood pigeon that perched on her chimney.

"Such a monotonous bird," she proclaimed once. "It is typical English. We would not 'ave zis bird in France."

"Ah," she thought. "That was in my early days here when I was bereft of aspirations."

Now she could boldly add an "h" to most of her words and of this she felt very proud.

Jacques was not so sure about the pronouncement on wood pigeons. He was sure he had seen one in the Bois de Boulogne and duly contradicted his aunt. She immediately bridled.

"It might have been a collar dove," he compromised, sensing her annoyance, for aunty invariably liked to be proved right.

Thinking of Jacques via the wood pigeon made her appreciate perhaps how much she missed him. She missed the Jacques of today, who was somewhere up north, and not the bumptious, precocious teenager that he once was.

But now she realised what it was that had awakened her as she ushered the soft swish of cereal slowly from its box. A revelation! That was it. And her thoughts of the old country confirmed it. A name change! The dream had hinted at it. It was the prelude, then, to the realisation of something she had long pondered.

She had lived in this country some time now and Dehoopney-Mer had given her nothing but problems, especially on the telephone.

Firstly, no one in the Passport Office in Peterborough had been able to spell her name and several times she had to return the documents.

"There is no "a" in Mer," she said crossly. "I am not an 'orse." Unaspirated, of course.

They were laughing at her; she could sense it. If not overtly, then there was a row of upper teeth biting bottom lip, as the clerks giggled silently on the other end of the line. Dehumpny-Mare had been the last straw!

"Can no one in zis town spell properly?" she complained.

"It is Peterborough, madam," said the receptionist.

"Alors," she replied, lapsing only momentarily into native speak. "I suppose it is maybe normal when you cannot say your town correctly."

"It is a city, madam" replied the receptionist. "We have a cathedral."

"It does not behave like a city. And it should be Peterburrow. Not brur!"

"It's but a minor problem," said the assistant, who was about to wheel off Costessey, Happisburgh and Wymondham (Norfolk variety) in defence, but thought better of it.

Even in France, they had remarked occasionally that her name sounded like a coastal resort, and some wag in the Post Office was always inserting a "sur" between the two names, to Etheldreda's protracted chagrin.

"No. A name change," she announced solemnly. "Ça suffit. I've 'ad enurf."

Moreover, it was time, she felt, to honour the country that had hosted her for the last twenty years. Yes, the same country with such illogical weather that prompted detailed and protracted conversation at bus stops. The country with its array of bewildering accents, or so she thought, which seemed to vary from one end of town to the other.

"Where was that man from?" she asked Jacques one day after an incomprehensible meter reader had paid a visit.

"Newcastle," said Jacques.

"I thought he was from Norway."

"Well that too. Originally, I suppose."

"I don't understand," she complained. "It is ridicule. No one speaks the same."

Jacques managed to suppress a smirk. Ever since he had discovered the word 'cul' in his dictionary, he had listened to some of his aunty's words in a new light.

"Ma langue. It is too rude sometimes," she lamented.

Then just when 'cul' seemed to have been forgotten, botany reared its unwelcome head.

"Why did you have to look zis word up?"

"It's only dandelion, aunty."

"That is better French."

"It's English, actually. And anyway, shouldn't it be "pissaulit" instead of "en lit"? Je suis au…"

"Oh, laisses ça!" she complained. It seemed wherever she looked ….

Then there had been the problem with her first name.

"Why Etheldreda?" she asked her own aunt one day.

"She was very likely French, anyway," came the reply.

"But she is a Saxon Princess. It is not logical."

Only persistence produced an answer she had little expected.

"Your dear parents were on holiday in England once."

"Yes…"

"Well, to cut a long story short, I think in all probability you were conceived in a cornfield in Suffolk. You were named after the church the postman went to."

"The postman…!"

"I'm afraid it was a major factor." The aunt giggled. "Alphonse, ton père, was unfortunately firing blanks, so this is where Harry from Exning stepped in." She paused briefly. "And that is why they decided to call you what they did, as a mark of respect and gratitude, most likely."

"It's too long a name," the niece replied, trying to overcome an unwelcome sense of shock and shame."

But now her mind was made up. She would announce the decision at Sunday lunch. It was a wise dream that had caused her to look at things anew, and a perceptive dream that emboldened her to rectify all the things that she felt unhappy with. She would tell them over the artichoke soup, which would serve as a prelude to the very appropriate roast beef.

"I have made up…" She paused for a moment. "..My mind, and it is time for change. For too long I have been saddled with this stupid name. It is both cumbersome and unwieldy. It gets me nowhere. No one can spell it and even the French laugh at me."

"Surely not?" said Cynthia, Jacques' girlfriend.

"Why 'ave two names when one suffit?"

"She means enough," said Jacques, translating for Cynthia.

"Well, I always thought it was a nice name. It had balance, well being…"

"Balance, mon cul," said the not for long to be Mrs. Dehoopney-Mer. "First of all, we need to shorten my first name. It is too long, too Saxon, too démodé. I will shorten it to Ethel."

"Are you sure, aunty?" Jacques asked.

"Absolutely," said Ethel. "My mind is made up."

"It's less of a mouthful, I suppose," he conceded.

"Precisely. Now for my second name, I have been looking at the English place names for inspiration."

"I thought you didn't like place names," said Jacques, remembering Peterborough.

The new Ethel ignored him. "I take my inspiration from the North. I have chose Ramsbottom."

Jacques spat out his soup.

"Eat properly, Jacques," said Ethel with distaste. And then in French "Essaies de manger proprement!"

"I am doing," he protested. "But I have to say it is not a wise choice."

"Mrs. Beddows from number twenty two went there on holiday. She said it was a most vibrant place. What's more, it sounds typically English."

"It was a snake on the Sooty show," volunteered Cynthia. "It had a very strong accent. I couldn't understand it."

"Aunty," said Jacques. "There's no way you can go from Dehoopney-Mer to
Ethel …"

"Tant pis!" replied Ethel, invoking part of the dandelion. "Just try and stop me."

It was at a gathering of friends and family, which was, by now, an annual event that Etheldreda decided to go public. Jacques had persuaded her against the imprudence of both the move and the announcement but with no success.

"I have to tell them. It is a major change."

"Won't you reconsider, aunty?"

"Absolument pas! It is better for me to tell them rather than 'ear it from someone else."

"I suppose so," conceded Jacques. "At least they're getting it from the horse's mouth."

Mrs. Dehoopney-Mer threw him a disapproving glare. "It is not very funny, Jacques. After all I have been through."

"I'm sorry, aunty. I was forgetting, of course."

"Yes. Forgetting! You are forgetting too much. It's too much time in that Dog and Duck nowadays. You are ruining your brain cells."

"I had fish last night, aunty. I could well be in credit."

"It is little in evidence," she replied.

There were twenty of them round the table that evening. Wafts of fine considered cooking had greeted the guests on arrival and they sat down eagerly to dinner.

"Are you all right, Jacques?" Henry Crispin asked as he arrived with his wife Mildred. "You look a bit peaky."

"I'm fine," said Jacques, only too aware of what was coming; of what was about to be unleashed on the unsuspecting visitors. "Just a bit of a late night."

"Ah well, you young people, you can cope with all that, I expect. When I was…"

"I'm sorry," said Jacques. "Can you excuse me a moment? I must just check on something in the kitchen."

Cooking was a comfort for Jacques in this troubled time. In fact, he would willingly have stayed in the kitchen all evening, although his absence would have caused some comment.

It was just after the lemon posset that Mrs. Dehoopney-Mer chose to rise from her chair. She tapped her wine glass with a spoon just as they do at weddings. Unfortunately, the spoon was slightly too heavy and, in her exuberance, the glass cracked down the middle.

"It's an omen, aunty," he whispered.

"Tais-toi, Jacques!"

He fell silent.

"Ladies and friends," announced Mrs. Dehoopney-Mer, trying a second glass.

"Shush!" said a voice in the background, at which the chatter subsided.

"As you all know, or maybe there are some of you who don't – though I expect from the generosity of your gifts and presence tonight – and I mean presence with a "ce"…"

There was mild tittering. She had cracked a joke. This showed some mastery of an otherwise elusive language with all its double entendres – but then that was French, wasn't it? She paused for a moment; the beaming smiles and courteous tee-heeing had given her a welcome surge of confidence.

"Er, as you know, I have now been in zis wise and wonderful country for some twenty years…"

There were nods of approval, then slight apprehension. Was she planning to return home across the Channel, or La Manche as some mischievously called it? Was this to be the last dinner? A whiff of melancholy hung over the remains of posset. To Mildred it seemed the colour had faded a little.

"In the beginning my accent was insupportable, execrable, as I'm sure you know."

Feeble protests of contradiction echoed round the table, although rather too feeble, she thought.

"But I was not to be resigned to this predicament, so I spent four weeks at St. Ogg's College."

Jacques was a little worried by this reference to St. Ogg's as, according to the Newtree Advertiser, it had doubled up in the evenings by entertaining wealthy businessmen, who indulged in a varied programme of indoor sports activities with unemployed Nepalese nurses. Fortunately, none of the visitors at table showed any recognition of the now humbled language school. It had surreptitiously closed and the mayor, who was also the language director, had resigned. It could also have been that auntie's otherwise impeccable pronunciation had dipped momentarily and that no one had noticed.

"My certificate is framed on the wall for all to see," she proclaimed.

Heads swivelled to where she was pointing.

"And so I gradually embraced the culture of my new host," she continued.

For some reason she had oddly omitted the word country.

"I learned to live without a mixer tap in ze sink, one of the strange phenomenons and perhaps failings of zis country. I learned to love my 'ot water bottle, except when it sprang a leak. I began to realise zat discussions on the weather were in fact covert messages of modulations and repressed rural inclinations..."

There was genuine bafflement.

"By my deep embracing of ze culture, I realised there was only one thing left."

Jacques quivered visibly.

"I needed to go one step further and to make myself part of the furniture. The chaise longue was to become a deckchair."

There was further puzzlement. What did Etheldreda mean?

"To do that, I realised I must change my name."

The assembly looked on intently.

"I wanted something I could identify with, that you all, my dear friends, could identify with. So, firstly, I have slightly abbreviated my first name. I have shortened it to Ethel."

"Hear, hear!" said a voice. It may well have been Harry Walters.

"Let's raise a glass to Ethel," said another voice. The likelihood was that it was Mr. Stirling Stone.

"Hear, hear!" repeated the first voice.

They all stood up and raised their glasses. "To Ethel!" they said.

Jacques perched against the table weakly. There was a rapturous round of applause. The guests sat down again.

"I think," continued the new Ethel, "it is important to define and associate oneself with a place. An English place. Therefore I have decided to choose and take the name of..."

There was genuine suspense and Ethel savoured the moment.

"Of Ramsbottom."

A shriek emanated from the end of the far table. Mildred had fainted.

There were confused snatches of conversation as the former Mrs. Dehoopney-Mer sat down to her new triumph. Mildred was being resuscitated in the library.

"Good on you, dear," said Harry Walters raising another glass. It may have been that he misheard. Mrs. Ramsbottom beamed.

"Well, I think that went rather well," she said later to an ashen-faced Jacques.

Her nephew failed to react, which she thought rather rude. However, he was all too aware of the consternation and confusion which ensued, and of which his aunt was blissfully unaware.

"Could he not have advised her?" a traumatised Mildred had enquired of him as she was being escorted home.

"I did try," he said. "But her mind was made up. She can be very determined at times."

"Yes," quaked Mildred, reliving the memory.

"Well, thank you, Jacques. It was a lovely evening," said Harry. He was always able to put a brave face on things.

"Thank you," winced Jacques.

Ethel glanced at her pale-faced nephew. "Are you all right, Jacques?" she asked.

"Perfectly, aunty."

"It's too much time in the pub," she observed testily. "You can be a little too English at times!"

"Yes, aunty."

Ethel closed her bedroom door and sat down contentedly on the bed. As she gazed out through the open window, beyond which the night had now fallen, a thought suddenly occurred to her.

What an inspired choice the name change had been! How wise and yet fortuitous. Taking a fountain pen from the drawer, she slowly inscribed her two initials on a piece of paper. Together they made an inspiring and impressive – she paused for breath – E. R. Just like those robust and perennial monarchs!

"Ah yes," she exclaimed, without a trace of accent. "What could be more English than that?"

The Uninvited

The kitchen was becoming difficult; moving from side to side. When she last came to see him, she talked about mobility; transferring. He recalled the face but couldn't place the name. Memory was an elusive commodity these days. A well meaning woman from the council; blonde, mid forties, earnest. He'd cracked a joke and it fluttered blithely by, past her nose, which was bent over the forms, and out of the window.

Many questions. Too many. She ticked boxes. June, that was her name. Her predecessor had been Julie. Confusing to have such similar names. You'd have thought they would have changed them for the convenience of the old folk.

Julie had been a pretty girl. He liked her.

"I want to stay here," he'd said to her. "I know it ain't perfect but it's too late to go to one of those shattered accommodations."

"Sheltered," Julie corrected him.

"I beg your pardon, dear?"

"It's sheltered not shattered. You said shattered."

"Did I? Well, we wouldn't want that, would we?"

"No, Arthur, we wouldn't," she said and squeezed his hand.

Pretty girl. She laughed a lot.

"You must have a young man somewhere," he'd said.

She tapped the end of her nose. "You look after Arthur," she said. "It's you who's on centre stage at the moment."

"Even so. There must be one somewhere," he replied.

Julie blushed ever so slightly.

"We'll do everything to enable you to stay here. But you've *got* to tell us. Tell us what's difficult and then we can look at any necessary equipment."

"It's good of you," said Arthur. "But I ain't got the cash."

"Don't you worry," she said. "Leave it to us to sort it out. Money's our problem not yours."

"Are you sure, dear? I mean, who's going to pay for all of this?"

"It's not your concern. There are grants."

"I don't want charity!"

"It's not charity," replied Julie. "You worked, didn't you? Paid your taxes?"

"That's true," said Arthur. "Paid for them all to have their fancy weekends. Gravy trains to Brussels, all expenses paid. I see what's his name's back in the Cabinet again. The one who got booted out. Back like a bleedin' boomerang. They've got no shame now. The old ones would have buggered off. But not now. And look at all that money they wasted on that bleedin' Dome. Millions! It's nothing more than an upside down saucer. A giant cowpat!"

Julie laughed and Arthur subsided.

"That was quite a speech, I suppose," he said. "They'll be buying me a soapbox next."

"I'm not sure we can run to that," replied Julie.

Arthur appeared confused. "But I thought you said money's…"

"I'm joking, Arthur. It was a joke. A small one, I admit. Not worth bothering about."

There was a pause. "Don't worry, you won't have to put up with them anymore."

"Why's that, dear? Is that this political correctness they're always talking about? Have you got to give the jokes up?"

"Hardly," replied Julie. "When that day comes…No, they're transferring me. This is my last visit."

Arthur sat back, crestfallen.

"Oh my! That is a shame. And I thought we were getting on so well. Why do they have to do these things?"

"Departmental reshuffle," said Julie. "Our manager."

"Managers," said Arthur. "Don't talk to me about managers! I had enough of that when I worked on the railways. People sitting around in armchairs. Wouldn't know one end of a train from another. They never worked on the railways. Draft 'em in from outside. And it shows! Those civil servants, they're just as bad. Do you remember that Beeching? Slashed the railways to ribbons."

Julie shook her head.

"I'm ranting again, aren't I?"

"You carry on, love. If it's good for your breathing, then don't let me stop you. Only make sure it doesn't put your blood pressure up."

"140 over 80," said Arthur proudly. "Here, you're talking like the nurse." He looked at her. "You'd make a good nurse, I think."

He couldn't say the same of the blonde box-ticker. She hardly looked at him as she assiduously shuffled her forms.

"Hypertension?" she said. "And…"

"Arthritis. My niece's daughter calls it Arthuritis. After me, you see."

He giggled. The visitor failed to laugh, turning back to the comfort of her boxes.

"It's bad for blood pressure," he said. "Puts the bugger up. My niece told me to drink vinegar each day. That's the mother of the little one. Cider vinegar and honey. Mix together. Nature's natural regulator. A remedy."

She was checking the forms again.

"What about my equipment?" he asked, wondering whether Miss. Baxter – that was the name he'd seen on her label – would take it as a double entendre. "She said I could have something for the bath."

"I don't know about that. That probably needs a separate assessment. I'll have to speak to my manager."

"Snakes alive!" Arthur exclaimed. "Julie used to arrange everything. How many technicians does it need to change a light bulb?"

"I don't know, Mr. Flanagan. I'm not an expert."

No, thought Arthur. Clearly not. It would be his pleasure to see her out. He saw her silhouette flit past the window outside; the sound of her footsteps going down the steps.

In the kitchen, the kettle had boiled and he lifted it slowly, painstakingly, wary of the hot liquid inside. It felt heavy. Perhaps he should have put less in, but then that might mean more visits to the kitchen, and his leg was hurting today.

Arthuritis! Ha! Where his wife Joan had come from, they talked like that, managing to elongate words like athlete into three syllables. He liked country accents; enjoyed them all. Even Brummie! When he listened to Wiltshire, he wanted to pee.

"That's not very nice," Joan had said. "What a way to talk about your nephew!"

"Not him," retorted Arthur. "The accent or dialect, or whatever you want to call it. The high notes, they make me want to wee."

"Everything makes you want to wee. That's too much Guinness, Arthur Flanagan. That's what it is."

"I suppose you never touch the stuff, dear," he'd said.

He sighed. Perhaps if she'd had more than one Guinness a month, she'd still be around today. They said Guinness was good for you.

His hands tugged at the curtain rail. It was dark after four now. It was miserable when they tampered with the clocks; put them back. He was never sure why they had to. Who wanted extra daylight early morning? And, more annoyingly, he had to reset all the timers, the electric alarm, the cooker. It played havoc with Mrs. Norris's body-clock at the corner shop. She said so each time the hour went forward or backward. What a strange thing time was! The railways had standardised it, of course. Brought the whole country together under one uniform time. It wouldn't do to have a different time in Birmingham or Derby, as there once was, when you're trying to run a service. Mind you, he thought, that way they'd never be late. They could fix or wangle the time so that these ramshackle companies that ran the railways now wouldn't have to stump up so many refunds.

No sooner had he sat down, than he noticed a crack between the curtains. It always annoyed him, curtain cracks, so he got up again.

Suddenly, as he leaned against the window, he gave a start. For a moment, he thought there was something out there, a shape under the solitary apple tree in the postage stamp garden. He took a deep breath and looked again. In the darkness, nothing seemed to be lurking there, but for a second...

It was that daft film that had done it! A musical about a car. As if! They had sought refuge in the Falmouth cinema on a day of holiday rain. Relentless! The cinema was a mass of dripping macs and puddles on the floor – not all, though, he thought, from raincoats.

He had fallen asleep in some gooey number and awoken to see a short, elfin man with a net. Was it the same film? Apparently so. The man in black with the elfin-shaped nose was called the Childcatcher. The nose was like a bloodhound's, designed to sniff out errant, petrified children. They would then be whisked away by this Pied Piper without a flute. It was daft, he knew, but the combination of suddenly waking and the strange story had given him dreams – nightmares. The ever present net seemed poised, waiting to ensnare...

There was nothing in the garden, no figures clad in black, so he sat back down, feeling the settee sink beneath him, and put on the radio for company. He poured himself his nightly whisky, normally letting it acclimatise to the temperature of the room and the glass.

"Sod it!" he said and downed it in one.

Two days later, there was a letter in the post. It was hand written on the envelope but bore the council logo. 'Developing sustainability' was the slogan above the postmark.

Looking at it for a moment, he wondered what on earth it meant. How could you do both? Surely one was moving, the other wasn't. It was a contradiction in terms.

Inside the envelope was a piece of paper signed by June Baxter. It was a copy of her box-ticking extravaganza that had been unleashed on him two days ago. At one point she had even asked him what time he got up in the morning. Cheeky so and so! As if it was any business of hers anyway! And then, did he have any visitors? People nearby?

"The Reverend Egworthy," he fabricated. "From number twenty two, Admiral Sir Hubertus Bulge. It was at the third name that the pen hesitated. Angelina Belladonna was perhaps too beautiful a name to be true.

"That'll do for visitors," June had said.

Pity, he thought. He was getting in full swing. "You asked me," he replied.

"Yes, I did," she said.

Perhaps they'd got off on the wrong foot, he thought. He could always behave better on the next visit, though the chances were it would be someone new and they'd have to start all over again. Even more box-ticking, most likely.

There was nothing else enclosed inside the envelope. No note, no compliments slip, nothing. It was no time for compliments, perhaps. No love lost between himself and the dour pudding that had knocked on his door two days ago.

He gazed out of the window at the now peaceful garden. It was lit by sunlight and the bark of the apple tree glinted with its melting droplets of frost. He sat by the window, taking in the sun. Julie had said there were vitamins to be obtained from its rays even through glass. So he would duly sit by the window, letting the warmth permeate through, squinting occasionally in the low winter sun reflected off the shed roof. Julie had said many things and he'd been willing to experiment, to try them out. In her unexpected transfer, he'd lost a friend, he felt.

Resolutely, he resisted the temptation to doze.

"Never in the mornings," he'd said to himself. "After lunch, yes. A siesta or post-prandial snooze was possible. But to sleep in the morning reeked of decadence."

It was during the afternoon that the doorbell rang. Miss Baxter, was his first thought. But she'd already been, he remembered. Perhaps there had been a box outstanding, or maybe she really was going to do something about some apparatus in the home. He moved as fast as he could and placed both hands on the latch. The door swung slowly open.

The shape outside was younger, enquiring.

"Carwash?" he said.

"Pardon?"

"You want me to wash your car?"

The youth was around eighteen or nineteen. Was he from Poland? Mrs. Ridgeway's plumber was and she said he was very good.

"No, thank you," said Arthur.

"Reasonable rate," came the reply. "I do better price."

"Thank you," Arthur repeated. "But I don't have a car."

The boy looked at him more closely, as if to suggest it was not normal.

No, I don't suppose you have, he seemed to say.

Arthur closed the door. Where had he been going, he wondered? Before the interruption. Ah yes, he thought. Call of nature.

In the evenings, when it was dark, he would sometimes use the garden if he was feeling too lazy to climb the stairs.

"Get a pot," Julie had suggested.

He declined on grounds of dignity.

"My neighbour uses a bottle and chucks it on the compost heap."

Surely the garden was too small to entertain such a feature.

"You know what I mean," she said.

He did.

He had nearly finished upstairs when the doorbell rang again. Some days, weeks even, nobody came, yet today he had a second call. It couldn't be the carwash boy as he'd already been. He tugged his zip quickly upwards and turned to head downstairs.

"Coming," he called from the end of the corridor, though it was unlikely that this would carry all the way downstairs.

The doorbell rang again; a more persistent ring, followed by a rap of the door knocker. This was often the postman's ploy, to do both, so he would need to get down there before the postman headed off. If not, a card would fly through the letter box telling him he had to collect it from the sorting office.

Arthur quickened his step.

It was then that something happened. Something went wrong and he felt himself sliding, falling, almost as if in slow motion; the hard inevitability of his full weight landing onto the frayed carpet. He felt something graze his right cheek.

It took him a moment or two to realise where he was. Perhaps he had lost consciousness for a while. The doorbell, he noticed, had lapsed into silence. The moment had gone.

But as he lay there, trying to regain his strength, he realised it was virtually impossible to get up. Each attempt left him feebler, more weary. His companion, the unvacuumed carpet, smelt of dust and tea. He tried to push himself up again, but his arm subsided under the weight.

He was angry with himself for hurrying. It had been foolish. Stupid! And that doorbell was probably not important. Not the postman. Not in the afternoon. More likely some persistent salesman wanting him to switch his gas supply!

He lay there for some time. It was growing colder now in his helpless position on the floor. The switch for the central heating was downstairs. His feet began to feel cool, then numb. Like a stranded whale, he lay there, wondering how long his rescue might be.

It could be a day or more. Days even. And he would become hungry too; thirsty. Arthur tried to call out but as he listened his voice seemed to have become smaller, insignificant.

As the last cry subsided, he suddenly thought he heard a click. He listened intently. There it was again. A door was being closed and there was the sound of someone coming up the stairs.

The shape was at the end of the corridor. He could make out the dark shoes, the cloak. In the right hand, something was being carried. It took a moment for him to realise what it was. The figure with the raised net came slowly towards him. Soft, stealthy treads.

He recognised it. The childcatcher.

Dominic O'Sullivan

Without Doubt

They were truly amazed how I got there. Really. They just couldn't believe it. All eyes, or nearly all, were raised above the podium, where I was casually suspended, happy in my perch of innocence. You'd think I was the original fun-spoiler, wouldn't you? Especially as they were having such a good time! They were almost getting the champagne out, the streamers, balloons. The spontaneous ovation was dead on cue, and then I slipped out quietly above the stage.

"How did that get there?" I heard one of them say. You can imagine how indignant I felt. That? I'm not a that! I'll show you what...!

"Security was stringent this year," I heard one of the faithful remark.

"Needed to be," agreed another. "In view of the way things are."

"Aye." Did my ears deceive me but was that a northern voice? In this place!

Anyway, it was quite easy. While all eyes were raised upwards and they were singing away, holding hands with tears of rapture and emotion, I slipped in. Noiselessly, soundlessly, my lithe shape caressing the plush blue carpets that had been paid for by all the grateful shareholders. I left no trace, no mark. Slid behind the mini wall adorned with plants in pots, then shinned up the curtain at the side, which rippled in time to the applause, lay in wait and pounced!

I suppose, on reflection, I've always had it bad; suffered from a bad press, that is. Honestly, you should see how I've been painted!

It's all down to Paradise, of course. That's it. The thing you aspire towards. The thing that's cracked up to be so cool and yet which accounts for so much misery down here. By the way, tabloids distorted that too. I see you shaking your heads. That kind of complacent, self-satisfied and dismissive smile when you decide those risible words are tainted with a lick of propaganda. Of course there were tabloids. Listening to saints was simply not enough. Inevitably, there were some committed to telling the truth but they soon got rid of them. As easy as that. Demoted. Scrapped. Said they didn't exist. So many of them fell by the wayside.

I tried to get them into a union. You must protect yourselves, I said. But the press subverted my so-called 'slimy' intentions. At which point, I have to say this. Another distortion. I'm as dry and smooth as polished wood. You know this and yet...

I'm sorry about that last statement. It slipped out suddenly. I'll retract it. This is certainly no time for animosity to sympathetic ears.

I was telling you about Paradise and I was asking, begging for your patience and understanding. You see, it just wasn't all it was made up to be. I know I've said that already but somehow the original idea got...well...lost. Sounds familiar, perhaps? Well, we all have our weaknesses, I suppose. The regime started getting a bit lax and there were various characters being put up into Paradise who really had no right to be there. It was the authorities down here who were partly to blame. They started selling plots up there, like a sort of heavenly time-share.

In the end, no one could remember who the original owners were and so it all got quite out of hand. Then, suddenly, power was seized by a very disreputable bunch of characters and they insinuated their way into all parts of the system. The trouble was the owner was too nice. Too trusting. Too kind. Wouldn't hear ill of anyone. I tried to whisper in his ear but he just became very angry and said I was stirring up trouble again, as usual!

It became genuinely quite sad because the place wasn't at all like it used to be. I know it wasn't exactly for me but it was sweet in a comforting kind of way. Lots of long hanging trees, drooping robes, people playing harps, sun, lakes and grottos. In the evening light they used to sparkle and the breeze brought the smell of jasmine and mimosa. There was the sound of a gentle sea, murmuring, murmuring…so softly, and we all slept well under the stars.

Then *they* took over. A bunch of bossy angels in a perennial flap. They started curfews and forbade street assemblies because they suffered from an insurmountable paranoia. Personally, I think they were hung up about sex. I mean, fancy not knowing what or where you are. It's very disorientating. Frankly, I've always known where I stand.

So one day, in a fit of xenophobic paranoia, because now they'd started to admit foreigners there, and, can you credit it, non-believers? You see, some of them were so good. They had impeccable credentials; they *had* to come in.

They rounded them up one sunny afternoon in one of the little chapels. You think that's gratuitous maybe, 'sunny afternoon' up there, but it wasn't all sunshine and roses. The time-switch on the rain machine wasn't working properly and sometimes it rained inadvertently during the day. They tried to blame that one on me. Always upsetting the applecart, they said. Appropriate, I suppose, but anyway this was on one of the days when it didn't go wrong and so everything was more convivial than usual. That only made it easier for them.

They swung their incense censers to hide the smell of gas that was seeping slowly, unnoticeably from the doctored candlesticks.

I, who escaped. Just me. I shot out through a hole in the brickwork. I, the lowliest of creatures. I fled that dreadful scene and surveyed it from my position on the hill. I was shaking all over, believe me. But who could I tell? Not a soul. No one would believe me. I of the poison tongue. And yet my distress was genuine.

The masked angels came out and they buried the bodies at sunset. I, who saw all this and could do nothing.

I see that you're looking rather glum or sceptical maybe. I had to tell you; to get my side of the story out.

Silence. Just silence. Let's listen to it now. That's it.

I feel a little better from all that and even if you don't believe me...well...

So from that time, I couldn't really believe in Paradise. I lost confidence in it; opted out. I mean, in the end, I wasn't entirely slung out, but I couldn't go along with it. It wasn't working. Didn't do what the label said. And since my rather undignified departure, there's been no news from up there at all. A total blackout. Nothing!

In retrospect, I think it worked better when there wasn't just one owner. There! I know I'll get panned for that! But truly, it did work out better when it was a sort of Co-op.

I see you shudder.

There were lots of little deities, small businesses, each responsible for their own patch. Not without competition, mind you! For each little deity tried to be nicer than the one next door. In a natural kind of way, of course. And if one god was getting a bit sycophantic, a bit too big for her boots, then the others would cut her down to size. In a fairly humble way, I hasten to add.

Oh yes, in the early days, there was a god on every street corner, in every wood and garden....

But gradually, everything became centralised and it was down to just one or two. A pity, really. There was something comforting in having an 'on the spot' deity. I know they didn't approve of me even then, but at least we knew where we stood. I was a bright spark once, as all the books will tell you.

Then one day they decided. Bring Paradise down to Earth!

I told them. I said it just won't work. Be off, thou low-life, they said! It was getting personal. Sour grapes, you party-pooper! But I knew it couldn't work, wouldn't, because I'd witnessed that scene, escaped from the horrors in the chapel; fled through the hole in the wall.

As time went on, there seemed to be an increasing need for Paradise. Each country wanted its own brand. It was so much in vogue. *The* thing! Some people had their doubts, the Russians, especially. Remember Zamyatin? Perhaps you don't. He certainly knew my worth. And H.G.Wells! Could see round corners, that man! "I am the spirit that ruffles the waters!" Very nice. That's what he said about me! And ruffle, such an elegant word!

But back to me. My little serpent body was a question shape, a puzzler. Now, in Paradise, there are no questions because, after all, there's nothing wrong. It's all sorted. Just nice exclamation marks that you get after Hosannas and Hallelujahs.

Anyway, as I was telling you when you came in; in the beginning. I shinned up the curtain just when they were approaching their climax. There were Hallelujahs and Hail Wondrous Something from all sides, so I slipped onto the Party slogan board and did my wilting impression of the pound sign. I'm not talking weights and measures here, as I'm sure you'll appreciate.

There were gasps from the blue rinses as I slunk into a serpentine posture of query, then back to the wilting pound. Just when they were about to start the beatification of their glorious leader! And out of tune, too! Have you heard the singing? It's not heavenly choirs of angels, I can assure you!

The incense was nearly wafting across the altar; hymns of faithful, ringing praise. The inconvertible, the resolute. And then the sermon fanatics saw my lissom shape and quivered.

I've done it all before, though. I hissed at the old vampire in Transylvania. He was well ahead in his construction. There were boos, too, of course, but I did what came naturally. I hissed and hissed. And in that moment of self-doubt, of incense-breaking revolt, he stumbled on his own altar and vanished from the screen. My first TV dissent! Marvellous! I can do it anywhere.

I've done most places really, from time to time. It's the thing I know best; was created to do. Where to next? Maybe across the seas. The Atlantic perhaps. They're all a little holier than thou over there. I can see they'll have need of me. I shall really have to spell it out, though!

I slip back above the podium, let my inquisitive tongue splay before me, sample the receding scent of incense for one last time, and take my final bow.

The Age of Enlightenment

"Well?" said Irma.

"Yes?" said Harry.

She put down her cup of tea. "Did you?"

"Afraid not," said Harry. "Fully booked."

"I *told* you!"

"I'm on the waiting list."

"Well, that's not good enough. You know how dim they are at that college. They can't tell arse from elbow."

Irma was always vulgar when she got annoyed. It was a warning sign.

"I did join another class, though."

Relief, clearly visible, flowed over her face. Harry was grateful too, as Irma's tetchiness was prone to lengthy spells. It was the right decision.

"Ventriloquism," he announced.

She promptly spat out the tea she was drinking. "What!"

"Ventriloquism."

"What on earth! Why? What were you thinking…?"

"It was the only one that had any places left. No waiting list."

"I'm not surprised. What a peculiar choice for an evening class!"

"It's the first year they've tried it. Said something about a pilot, though I'm not sure where he comes in."

Irma threw him an odd look. "It may well be the last."

"I thought you'd be pleased. You're always talking about a challenge. I'm sure the people'll be very interesting."

"Undoubtedly. But why not something else? What about a foreign language? Or pottery, maybe?"

"They're all booked up. And they only do Spanish now."

"What happened to French?"

"It appears that Mrs. Beaune hasn't come back from holiday with Jim the college gardener. It may not be taking place at all now."

"And when does it start, your ventriloquism course?" Irma asked, looking to the future.

"September 18th," he said. "All paid up and ready to go."

Irma seemed a little brighter.

Every Tuesday Harry would set off eagerly to Lindfield College in time for the seven o'clock class.

"Better eat before I go, dear," he'd said. "We won't be able to hold out till half past nine."

"As you like."

"Perhaps, though, I'll take a sandwich for later. Just in case."

Harry liked the twenty minute walk along the leafy avenues to the run-down and partly dilapidated annexe of Lindfield College. As a bonus, Ron, his former railway colleague had joined the class too. Together they paired up for the introductory deep breathing exercises.

"Deep, deep breaths," the instructress said. "Imagine you are whales on the high sea. There, hold it for longer." Her arms were round Harry's chest. "And...exhale!"

"She's a bit strict," Ron confided as they went for a healing pint afterwards.

"My sides are sore," grumbled Harry. "And no jokes about..."

"She said it would wear off after a while," said Ron. "There's often a lot of suffering involved in true art."

Harry chose to ignore Ron's observation. He drank meditatively at his beer.

"Did your Hilda mind you coming to these classes?"

"Not really," said Ron. "She freaked out a bit at first. What's wrong with French, she said. I pointed out it was a little dispiriting to be a beginner for more than five years."

"Surely you can go up after the end of each year?"

"No," said Ron. "Cos at the end of the summer holidays I've forgotten the bloody lot and I have to start again. Hilda says I have the retentive powers of a goldfish, whatever that means."

"There is no French," said Harry, "because Mrs. Beaune ran off with the one-legged gardener."

"Really," said Ron. "Well, that leaves hope for all of us. Amor vincit omnia."

There was a stunned pause.

"Perhaps I should have done Latin."

"Enjoy the class, dear," Irma enquired when Harry staggered in at half past eleven."

"Very good, thank you."

"I see you're not too steady on your feet."

"All those breathing exercises," he answered.

"I see. And did the class continue at the Rose and Parrot?"

"Ron's suggestion," said Harry. "He's feeling his way after all those years of French. It came as rather a shock. And it's thirsty work, dear. We were both quite parched afterwards."

When the clocks went back, Harry negotiated the leaf-strewn pavements in darkness.

"Take a torch, dear," suggested Irma.

"It's got no batteries."

"Like you, dear," she murmured. "Well, why not get the bus?"

"No," said Harry, resolutely. "I enjoy the walk. It gives me a chance to do all my breathing exercises. It's very useful."

"Just so long as you don't scare anyone on the way. It's bad enough with those joggers groaning and grunting when you're out shopping."

"Yes, dear."

"Will you be going for a drink afterwards?"

"I should think so."

"It's their Polynesian evening tonight."

"How do you know?" asked Harry, surprised.

"Full page ad in the paper."

"Really! It's a tough time for locals at the moment."

There was a long pause during which Harry felt he was under scrutiny.

"Er, you wouldn't like to come along, dear, would you? We could make up a foursome with Hilda."

Irma thought for a moment. "No," she said. "It'd cramp your style. I wouldn't want to intrude on your field of pleasure. You go and enjoy yourselves."

By the end of the course, Harry was doing reasonably well. He had even achieved some of his ambitions.

"You are projecting your voice well," said Carlotta as Harry was holding forth in conversation with a tea cup.

"Thank you," he said.

"But you need a little more work on your plosives."

"I do?" he replied, wondering what she meant.

"And now it gives me great pleasure to hand out your attendance certificates."

There was a buzz of anticipation in the dimly-lit hall. Eight participants advanced slowly to receive their treasured documents. There was rapturous applause after each one.

"Er, what about mine?" whispered Ron to Carlotta.

Miss Da Capo consulted her register. "I'm so sorry," she said, "but there was a period of absence in May. The college stipulates an attendance of eighty per cent."

She looked momentarily severe in her new glasses.

"That was when the cat was ill," protested Ron.

"I'm sorry," she replied, "but the college is quite clear about this."

"Oh well," said Ron. "I can always have a go again next year."

"Ah." Carlotta Da Capo looked thoughtful. "I regret the course won't be running next year."

There was a collective gasp of disappointment. A cloud had settled over their prized certificates.

"The college has decided it is not vocational enough, and, in addition, the number of participants enrolled was rather small. But it has been a pleasure to work with you all."

"I'll say," said Ron, who particularly liked Carlotta's hands around his waist when he was doing the Green breathing exercise.

"We'll miss you," he sobbed as he planted a kiss on her powdery cheek.

"As I will you, my dears," she said.

Over the summer, Harry and especially Ron seemed rather subdued. It was as if the sun had disappeared behind a giant cloud; after illumination came darkness.

"At least he won't have all those marks round his midriff," said Hilda when she met Irma out shopping. "Makes you wonder what went on in all those classes. Still, he's not been the same since they finished."

"It was nice too," said Irma, "to have him out from under my feet in the evening. I managed to finish painting the patio."

"Did you, love? I wonder what they'll do next year."

"There's a course on meditation, I believe. And I gather Mrs. Beaune has split up with Jim the gardener."

"I thought it had to be vacational," replied Hilda.

Irma hadn't the heart to correct her.

It was a hot afternoon in August and Harry was sitting in his shorts under the shade of the apple tree. Irma was asleep in the adjacent chair, wasps hovering near the fallen apples beneath. His gaze traced the curves of her ample bosom. She was wearing that frock he liked. And as for Irma's auntie, she had had the most fabulous…

Irma suddenly opened her eyes to see Harry staring at her.

"These wasps are a nuisance," she said.

"Let's go inside, dear. It'll be cooler there."

He was right. Even in the bedroom, the westerly sun had not yet reached the upper windows.

"Put some sun cream on my neck, will you, Harry? It feels quite sore."

"Yes, dear," said Harry. He had a sudden glint in his eye; a glint of old that Irma recognised.

"You can cut that out," she replied. Too much sun made her grumpy.

"Do you remember how it was in your dad's house, when we used to sneak upstairs while he was cutting the lawn? I was grateful to that mower. It used to drown out…"

"Yes," said Irma remembering and feeling her neck. "Then he'd come back in. Always at the wrong moment. And he'd call out to us, too."

"Anyone fancy a brew oop there?"

The flat-vowelled monotone that Harry mimicked seemed to come from beyond the room but just outside the door. Irma was amazed.

"Joost comin'." This was Irma's voice now.

She looked at Harry. There was a smirk all over his face.

"Is that what you learnt in those classes?" she asked. "You and Ron?"

"Yes. Well, no, not exactly." He was taking off his shorts. "But there's plenty more."

"I hawpe there's naw bloody hanky-panky gawin' on oop there."

A deep northern baritone was now drifting across the landing.

"Ooh," said Irma, matching Harry's visible excitement. "Ooh, come here you great…"

She dragged him onto the nearby bed.

"What about the sheets?" he asked considerately.

"Bugger that!" she gasped. "Just come here!"

Most afternoons now, it seemed, the curtains would slide across the upstairs bedroom windows of number forty-two Melchett Drive, where the house would resonate with a plethora of voices and a full range of English vowels.

At Christmas, Miss Da Capo was delighted to receive a card and letter from an appreciative Harold. In addition to sending greetings to her island holiday residence, he wondered if there was any possibility of attending a follow-up course. He and a number of other retired gentlemen would be quite prepared to go privately. Money, no object! They were very interested!

Late Call

It's turned cool now after a day of rain and I can sense those eyes still upon me. I go to close the last window, just slightly, and a whole cascade of rain falls from the tilting glass. In one deft movement I put the rest of the papers in my briefcase, click it shut as quietly as I can and mumble an inaudible goodbye.

I am out of the room before he can see me, gliding down a newly Ajaxed corridor. In the car park, Morris Minor - sounding like a pupil - is waiting obediently for me. I glance in the mirror but he has not followed me. The ignition's squawking like a rattled hen and I am lurching tentatively down the drive.

Back home, something's gone off in the fridge and, as usual, there is a choice of suspects. As I gaze inside, the shelves appear lonely after a day's work. I decide it's the speckled cheese - the one I never really liked – so I toss it into the pedal bin. After a few minutes, I change my mind and escort the stinking cheese downstairs in a carrier and banish it to the dustbin.

It rains all over the weekend. Rain. No prizes for guessing that Monday'll be fine.

A breeze is blowing gently. My prediction was right; it's a glorious day and I'm standing out in the fresh air to a smell of damp grass. Everything's well organised. There's even a white coat to make me look the part. The pitch, however, is on a slope and by the far line of trees, there's a muddy stream. I anticipate several journeys made in that direction, foraging hopelessly through beds of nettles. To the spectator, and some drift in, it must look a pleasing sight. A squad of pale-clad figures ambling over a sea of green. There's a haze, too, beyond the willows, so maybe the ball will swing today.

It's 58 for 5 and slow progress when he comes out to bat. He's asking me a question - the first time I've had to notice him today - a direct one, a technical one.

"Middle and leg?" he asks. I don't even have to reply with words. The outstretched fingers, which were holding the pebbles previously, wave him back and he steps a little to the left. But when he waits for me after class, the questions are more involved and it's difficult to run. I wonder whether I'm appearing off-hand. Have the others seen? No, they're probably not even noticing.

He quickly strokes the ball around - a skilful gladiator - and with the last boundary he's all smiles. They should have sent him in earlier, but then perhaps it's wiser to keep your best things in the cupboard till last. He looks a natural with the bat; the sun shining off his golden hair. But as I glance up there's a scream in my ear and the ball is thudding off his pads. The field goes up. The appeal is confident. I hesitate. I know you're supposed to give the benefit, but I'm anxious that... I'm not making sense, I know. The next thing that happens is that my finger's raised. The team is celebrating. Ben stands for a second in disbelief and slowly walks off. As he passes me at the set of stumps, his eyes flicker for a second. Is there a semblance of a scowl? A sneer, maybe?

There's a ripple of applause from the pavilion. He was going well and now it's over. I finished it. I. For the greater good, you see.

After the game's over, I slink back shame-faced to school.

I think about it for the rest of the week. What might have been? A fifty? A hundred even? But fortunately there are no more Games. The weeks drift off into the realm of exams. It'll get hotter, you'll see. No scheduled lessons now, no waiting for me after class.

When the term finishes it's a weight off my mind. For two months I'm free and up to date with everything. I'm going to go on day trips, explore the area, so I'm off to Silverton on Sea. I'll take the train - it's only a short ride. A few pints on the promenade. No need to drive. Take myself off along the cliffs if it's fine.

But when I get there, the place is swathed in cloud. It's a bit murky but maybe it'll clear. When I walk along the High Street, with its unruly row of shops, it seems to get brighter already.

"It's the sea-fret," the park attendant says. "Sometimes it goes, sometimes stays all day. It's higher up here though, that's why it's better."

The park is gradually bathed in a sickly, milky light. I stroll round a lake of disgruntled geese. My bag is almost empty, contains no food, so eventually they honk and then turn their backs. I look at the line of boats assembled outside a pavilion. Strange there should be so many, while out at sea there's nothing, not even to the misshaped island, which I later learn is a sanctuary for birds.

It's as I turn that it happens. He sees me. I'm confused seeing another world in an unsuspected place.

"What are you doing here?" he asks me.

He's out of school clothes; tee-shirt, light flannel trousers.

"I could ask the same of you."

There's a brief silence.

"Just thought I'd take a day out. Get to see what there is."

He shrugs indifferently."Just sea."

"And you?"

"I'm working on the boats. It's my summer job. I've done it the last three years."

He smiles. He's forgotten my transgression on the cricket field. Or has he?

"Fancy a boat?" he says. "Take as long as you like. It's my uncle's place."

"No thanks," I mumble. "I'm not very good at rowing."

On hearing my excuse, he's all ears.

"That's all right. I can take you out later when we finish. Six o'clock?"

The last train from Silverton goes at ten past seven, but all I can do is nod.

"Come back later," he says. "I'll take you round."

"See you later," I say.

As I walk round the long and twisting lake, my stomach's full of butterflies, fluttering sensations. How will I get back later? Taxi maybe, or stay in a B&B? But all this seems unimportant as I look out onto the lake over which I shall be floating later.

The sea fret lifts. I drink two pints of beer. There's a strange eggy taste to it. Supper's fish and chips served out of a newspaper. The Weekly Herald. The High Street shops have closed. The clutter of buckets and mops that spill out of their open doors are all inside. Maybe it never happened. The park seems empty. The world's at tea.

"There you are, sir," says Ben. "I'll just be a few minutes and we can go out."

He looks appealing in white flannels.

I've only taught two years.

The way he pushes the boat out and grabs the set of oars makes him look a seasoned professional. Mind you, I'm an easier crowd to control. Just me in the boat.

We drift off, past from the boathouse, and Ben's arms are pulling at the oars. I gaze at them, golden brown and bronzed in the fading sun and wind. They must be strong from all that practice.

And now he's bobbing back and forth in front of me, legs outstretched. I glance towards him. I enjoy the rhythmic swaying motion and respond accordingly.

He grins as we scatter the birds that are in our path as he mischievously follows them. Even if I were to disapprove, birdwatcher that I sometimes am, I can do nothing. I am captive of the lake and its waters that appear too deep to jump ship.

"We'll take a look at the island," he says, as I spy a straggly line of willows leaning down to the water's edge.

I've only taught for two years.

There's nothing I can do. The last train will be leaving as I limply follow like some kind of sheep. As we disembark onto the island, the ground feels soft and gentle.

And I can see the last train going, see it leaving now; a puff of diesel smoke blowing into the oncoming darkness.

Out of Sight

"It's agreed, then," she said. "You'll go?"
"Yes."
"To the library?"

He nodded. She sank back among the pillows, piled high like mountains of snow.

"Is it cold outside?" she asked him.

Gerald went to the window. He himself hadn't seen the day outside yet. Towards the end of the lawn was a sprinkling of frost; a dusting of icing sugar.

"It seems so," he said.

She smiled. "I remember how when you got up in the morning there used to be ice patterns inside the windows. Like the curtains they had at cinemas; intricate forests of silken trees."

"Central heating," he said. "Unheated rooms then."

Monica nodded. She understood the connection.

"Would you like some more tea?" he asked her. "You know, before the carers come?"

Monica raised herself to look at the clock. Was there time?

"I think there is," he said, reading her thoughts, interpreting her sudden leftward movement. "I'll go and make it."

He took the tray with the single glass of water downstairs. Bubbles had formed around the edges overnight, making it look like some kind of health drink. He refilled the glass and put the kettle on. On the mat, the post had come; various rectangles of white splayed across the floor.

He was on the pier. A wind was blowing. Through the gaps in the wooden slats, the waves frothed angry and foamy. If a large wave battered in, the pier seemed to shake and shudder for a few seconds as it took the full force of the impact. He liked those moments and wondered what it would be like if the pier was cast adrift into mid ocean. An unlikely, preposterous island of uniform benches, canvas deckchairs, fruit machines and toilets, floating, wandering out to sea.

Gerald smiled. It was on one of those benches he had first met her. She sat stoically facing the gusting wind, shoulders upright, back perfectly rigid; not a slouch anywhere to be seen. Perhaps it was the posture he had first noticed, then the face beneath the headscarf; the startlingly vivid blue colour of her eyes. They had talked for a few minutes. Pleasantries. Commented on the weather.

"We need the sea," she'd said.

At the time, he'd never really asked her what she meant, but sort of guessed. The words stayed with him.

"It's chilly," he said. "Should we go in for a cup of tea?"

"Sounds like a good idea," she said. She got up slowly, as if it was a giant, meaningful step.

The café was only a few feet away. Almost deserted. Two hangers-on by the far windows, gazing out to sea. The coffee machine hissed and spluttered, as if some vast aquatic creature was thrashing about inside, or they were at some preserved railway station which dealt in steam trains.

They chatted till closing time, until the last chairs were piled rudely high on the remaining tables. They met again on the pier, and again; told stories, traded anecdotes – widow, widower. Rocky, the first marriage of his to Joanna. Like a ferry listing on high seas. She smiled. She had forsaken the headscarf. She looked radiant.

He took the tray upstairs. The cup and glass were touching each other, both vaguely aware of the other's existence; they chinked and wobbled as he carried it up. The room was quiet again. Monica lay asleep, her face clenched inwards in a silent contortion of pain. Then the eyebrows gradually relaxed and she opened her eyes.

"You haven't forgotten?" she said.

"No, dear." There was a pause. "The library."

"And you checked the times?"

"Yes. Late night closing."

"Good."

He smiled to himself.

"What's funny?" she asked.

"Late night closing. Makes it sound like a supermarket or one of those discos. Something happening."

I'd send you there if need be, she thought.

A cloud of pain returned and she was hidden, buried beneath that cloud.

When the carers left, two strong-docked women from Bristol, he followed the prescribed timetable. He dusted the front room, though there was little dust to speak of. More often than not, he sat out in the back.

He waved an amber cloth over the polished wooden furniture. Outside in the street, a small girl on her mother's arm waved back. They both waved.

"Not waving," he said to himself, "but…"

He couldn't bring himself to say the last word. It would be too…

He cleared the breakfast table, carefully scraping off a dollop of marmalade that had fallen onto the cloth; made them both a drink…went upstairs.

"You *will* go?" she said later that afternoon. "You won't just sit around downstairs."

He nodded. "No."

"There's always the risk that you might be seen."

I could draw the curtains, he was about to say. Draw them tight.

"It's important," she said.

"I know," he answered.

"I'm thinking of you."

Of course she was, so he nodded again, even though instinct suggested the other way.

"It *has* to be this way," she said. "No repercussions."

The curtain shifted in the slight breeze. He went to close the window a little. She stopped him. It didn't matter now.

Repercussions! What a beast, what a rumpus of a word, he thought! There were noises, clashing sounds and havoc within. Recriminations. It seemed to run into repercussions. They would combine their forces together.

At six o'clock, he held her hand and kissed her. A long time. Everything was on the table as she'd specified. He looked at the assembled objects for one last time then back towards her; their strategic positions were like pieces on a chess board.

He wasn't to linger, she'd said. He had to go. Her quiet breathing told him that. The front door clicked mechanically, coldly behind him.

He pictured her upstairs.

Tears all the way to the library now, where Miss Pritchard was waiting. She walked a few steps with him; touched him lightly.

"I've kept a table free."

Reservation, he thought and almost laughed – would have laughed if it weren't so bitter. It made the place sound like a restaurant. The reading room, a restaurant! The world turned upside down!

"There are a few of the papers. Yesterday's. I kept them under the counter. Today's are still out, I'm afraid."

"What about the camera?" he asked. "Won't it pick them up?"

"No," she answered. "I don't think so. It's not that clever. Besides, you're entitled to read yesterday's papers, aren't you?"

"Yes," he said. "It's just Monica thought of…"

He remembered libraries before cameras – most places, come to think of it.

"We are the most spied-on nation," Sheila Mowbray, the senior librarian, had said to one of her underlings in a late evening debate once. Gerald stopped what he was reading and listened but took no part.

"Nineteen eighty four was too early," Sheila continued. "Orwell got it wrong. It came later with this lot."

"Who's Orwell?" he heard the assistant reply.

There was a sudden rush of stunned silence. Miss Mowbray didn't reply. He could picture her, gasping inwardly. She left it to the silence.

"I'm taking a break at quarter to seven," Miss Pritchard whispered. "I've told them here I had a shorter lunch so I won't be back till quarter past."

He nodded almost imperceptibly. It felt like they were taking part in a conspiracy; that he and Miss Pritchard were conversing as lovers.

"Are you really sure you want to do this?" he asked her.

"I have to," she said. "Someone must be there. I promised."

Yes, you did, he thought. You and Monica. Unbeknown to me…

"It won't just be me there," she whispered.

A head turned in their direction.

"You *know* that!"

Gerald lowered his head. It was too much! Unspeakable!

"You'll be there. A huge part of you... will be there... with me."

She paused. "And I'll tell you. Just ask me... afterwards. I'll..."

She was right, of course. Nearly all of him would be there. The glass of water. The neat pile of tablets.

The shabby raincoat he sat in covered an empty husk. There he was now with Wilma Pritchard, entering the house, fumbling with the keys before entering, climbing the staircase, sitting now on the other side of the bed as she held Monica's fading hand.

"I'm on my break now," he heard Wilma announce to the remaining staff.

There was a grunt of recognition, then the swish of the library's revolving door. She would be out on the street; out in the colder air. Wilma had parked a few roads away so the staff wouldn't be able to hear the unmistakeable spluttering of her car in the librarians' car park.

He was walking with her to the car. The key slid in the lock; the lights came on, illuminating a fine drizzle. He heard the levers inside clunk and click, or whatever they did.

But what if it wouldn't start? Cars didn't like bad weather. So what if...? There wouldn't be time for her to walk there and back. She could run perhaps! For peace of mind, maybe, he should have seen her off; seen her sailing down the avenue; trees turning into dark shapes in the encroaching twilight.

She would park the car at the bottom of the road, then walk up and let herself in. The house would be silent but she might notice the tinkling of the clock in the living room when she passed by.

She was climbing the stairs now. The tray would be empty; everything taken; water drunk.

Something came from within him; a gasp followed by a shudder. The realisation.

It was so wrong. He *should* be there! *Should* have been there!

He got up quickly from the chair, sending the paper flying. As he reached forward blindly to gather the pages together – he couldn't leave them splayed across the floor – he could hear Monica's voice.

"At no time must you be here, in the house… when it happens. You understand that?"

He tried to protest, to dissuade.

"They would say that you were involved. Complicit. They would say that you *helped* me."

She was doing it for him, she said. For both of them.

"The law…it can't be altered. Cannot…"

"But to be alone," he said, "when it happens!"

"I've thought of that," she said. "Alone, yes. That's how they'll see it. But not completely."

"Not completely?"

"There is someone who'll come."

He was confused. "But won't they think it funny if I'm sitting up in the library?"

"You weren't to know what would happen. What was going to happen. My state of mind…"

"But I did! I did! You told me. They'll ask me."

"Then you say that you didn't. You knew nothing. You lie."

There was a silence.

"Wilma will help you," she said.

"Wilma?"

She explained carefully what she'd arranged. They'd got it all worked out. Wilma would be there keeping watch for a time, during her 'break' from the library. And he would be in the reading room, poring over papers; captured on camera.

"Captured on camera," he'd said to himself. "Captured." The phrase stuck in his head like the title of a book or poem. 'Eyeless in Gaza', 'Captured on Camera'.

He glanced up at the clock, which showed five past seven. It was a library clock. It wouldn't strike; time was silent here.

"And don't look at it," said Monica, meaning the clock. Don't look as if you're waiting for something. You must sit as if nothing was going on."

He stared around him. A room where grief would have to be kept to a minimum. The camera may not detect silent tears, but sobs…

It was nearly half past seven when he heard Wilma return to the library desk.

"I'm sorry I'm late," she apologised. "I just had a call on my mobile."

Mobile. Yes, mobile. She'd thought of everything! A library call would have shown up as a light on the large white phone.

"Everything all right?" her colleague asked.

"Well…" Wilma's answer was suitably vague, tapering away into non-committal evasion. It drifted further away over the shiny floors.

She was studiously ignoring him. He sensed it. As agreed, they wouldn't speak until five to eight, when she would come into the reference section and announce that the library was closing.

The minutes were like the movements of a sloth; barely detectable. It seemed an age before they elapsed.

At five to eight, precisely, the doors of the reading room concertinaed open.

"We're closing in five minutes," Wilma Pritchard said perfunctorily.

He offered some kind of stumbling reply.

Afterwards, they would talk together in the pub across the way. It was rumoured they had CCTV. So much the better.

Would she say it was peaceful, he wondered?

He could hear the outside doors being locked. The caretaker would stand in the entrance now to prevent any latecomers from entering. He heard the sliding down of bolts. The doors would be temporarily unlocked to enable those within to leave.

It was nearly over.

Voices in the Dark

"It's your turn," O'Hagan said as he was off to watch the rugby. "There won't be many of them. Not at all. Sport always takes precedence over the needs of the soul."

Donal McMartin was not so sure. He always felt nervous about doing it as the penitents tended to congregate when he was on. Moving through the semi-darkness, he became slightly anxious as he approached their silhouetted shapes. O'Hagan was wrong. There they were waiting in two long rows, their faces lit up by the flickering candles. For a moment, he looked away to a distant corner so as not to recognise them. It was usually better that way.

Opening the creaking door of the box, he stepped inside. A solitary little one-bar fire stared sadly back at him and at that moment the thought flitted across his mind, 'What if you don't work?' The radiators in the church had been off since Sunday, making it colder than usual, so he flicked the switch and waited. There was no sound except for the footsteps on the other side of the partition. Someone was inside.

As he listened intently, he kept an eye on the radiant, waiting for it to turn from bright orange pink to amber. But as the voice began to whisper behind the grille, nothing happened and he started to shiver on the cold bench. Suddenly he remembered something and felt inside his pocket. There, indeed, was the reward; a pair of reliable thermals which had been stuffed hurriedly into a pocket as a contingency measure. He unfolded them eagerly, absolving the voice that had now left the box, slipping one shoe off then another.

Concentrate, will you! He was being addressed again, and for a second, a foot dangled precariously on the icy stone floor. Wincing briefly, he agilely slipped one sock on, hoping that whoever was on the other side would attribute any noises to heavy contemplative breathing. After the necessaries and an interlude of reflection, the voice again departed, and now, with both thermals padding his toes like boxing gloves, he wiggled his feet back into his shoes. Feeling more comfortable, he sighed gently and sat back to listen. A loud voice was now shaking the confessional, indirectly addressing the alarmed penitents outside.

"I'm only just here," Donal whispered to the voice. "Otherwise they'll hear you down at the railway station!"

The voice carried on regardless and impervious. Following absolution, the door closed. Silence now and temporary tranquillity! And in the peaceful silence another less familiar noise. There was a loud hum, followed by an intermittent buzzing. A couple of sparks shot out of the side of the bar. The electric fire had finally decided to switch itself on.

Donal remembered that Sister Mathilda had a record player like that once. When all was forgotten and abandoned, a phantom arm sneaked across the deck and dropped the record down all on its own with a deafening clud. Some things were definitely not meant to serve man, he pondered. They acted independently on erratic whims.

A light wafted up from the fire and from his side a cheery glow made the wood appear shiny in the gloom. This time he was being spoken to softly, very softly, for some while by a hushed, penitential voice. In between the gentle whisperings, he heard the church clock ping. His feet nestled snugly in their socks. The voice murmured on, developing its indiscretions at great length. Surely it was time...? It was warm; the smell of polish coupled with incense and the ticking of the clock...

Suddenly, he was alert to something. The fire was sparking, spitting, turning itself off again. His eyes felt heavy and then... He looked up anxiously. Beyond the grille there was utter silence; no one. Or was there? He coughed, cleared his throat. Moving nearer, he peered more closely. No, the box was now quite empty. As he ventured outside, his eyes fell on the rows of vacant benches.

Oh no, he thought. Oh no!

The church clock ticked spitefully showing half past seven. And through the darkness, he could gradually make out a small, half-crouching shape. It was the familiar backside of Mrs. Mc.Bay who often cleaned on a Saturday.

"I've just switched off the porch lights now, father, and tidied up the vestry."

In the dancing candlelight, her cold, clear eyes seemed to penetrate right through him. Feeling awkward and embarrassed, he looked away.

"I'd better unplug the fire," he muttered and stepped momentarily back into the safety of the confessional. He rubbed an anxious finger around his collar. His neck was damp with anxious perspiration. He had the sensation that she was staring at him, her eyes fixed upon him in the half-light. On the nearby stand, the last candle flickered and went out.

"Father O'Hagan never uses that fire," Mrs. Mc.Bay announced from somewhere down the darkened aisle. "He never uses it at all. In fact, he says it's unreliable. Does all sorts of tings."

And as she gave the statue of Saint Boniface a final flick of her duster, he retreated humbly, chastened and forlornly into the welcome anonymity of darkness.

The Pump

It was just after the factory siren had shrieked out beyond the reservoir that the pump stopped working. George Carter looked from his upstairs window with bewilderment as he heard it grind to a soft whirr and then lapse into silence.

This was only the second time it had done this. Before, he remembered a few last bubbles slowly making their way to the surface then all was silent. Quickly he put on his coat to go towards the spot where the trouble might be located.

Stupid thing! Unreliable! Why didn't they get a new one? Anne Marie had always said.

It was perhaps not as fickle as she imagined.

At that point, he stopped dead in his tracks. It was maybe the tenth time today he had thought of her. Inevitable. No alternative. There were too many connections, too many sounds. Try as hard as he liked, it would be impossible to remove even a third of all these associations.

"Why don't you move on?" Joe had suggested. "Get a transfer. Somewhere more scenic. Start again."

It was easier said than done, of course.

Naturally they had all been very sympathetic when it had happened. The whole workforce. No end of sympathy.

"Don't come in for a week or so," Riley had said. "Take your time. We can get a relief."

That was all he needed. Hours of emptiness, of awkward sympathy, when what he needed was work, long hard work. Something to bombard and tire the senses with. Either that or else get away – right away. Never come back to this place, a voice within him murmured.

He couldn't. It was impossible. He sat in that small ugly house all day beyond the last of the reservoirs, his window shielded by the branches of an ash which filtered the late afternoon sun. Beneath were the last few offerings of the vegetable patch, discarded, unwanted and turning now to seed.

He had got up late. Dreaded it... Leaves of winter sprouts waving up and down, as memory appeared and reappeared like some kind of endless wheel...back and forth, back and forth.

If only he hadn't gone. Taken himself to the White Horse while Anne Marie climbed the stool that led to the cupboard containing the elusive bowl... Shifting his dominoes on the wooden tables of the half-empty pub, putting down his double four, at probably the same moment that Anne Marie fell. Fell, slipped, fell!

It must have been during the third game, he reflected afterwards. The third, third! And as he played, he cast occasional glances at the clock because Anne Marie didn't like being in on her own in the late autumn evenings.

It was eerie in the isolated house with no neighbours and the ticking of the kitchen clock. Beyond the window, the habitual November mists drifted slowly across the silent waters, obscuring everything. Sometimes she used to count the apples in the backroom, brought in from the garden, and place one upon her apron, rubbing it gently, polishing it with a cloth.

But this was enough. He saw Anne Marie fall, as if in slow motion, fall as he sat nursing his glass in the smoke-ridden pub. And today, for only the second time, the pump had completely stopped.

He picked up the phone, put it down again.

Realised he hadn't inspected properly... hadn't *really* been out.

There was hogweed growing in the vegetable patch; large leaves like an overblown marrow or maple, as he trod the stony path.

George bent down to take a closer look, his knee scraping against the side. Sure enough, the pump had stopped.

A gull was circling overhead. The lakes were popular with them in the winter months. A second dived into the water.

And there it was, sheltered under a giant metal canopy, black, vast and cumbersome... the silent machine. For a moment or so he ran his fingers over the greasy metal. He'd never been that good on pumps, unlike some of the other workers, and least of all with this one. It was supposed to be pumping from the top to the lower reservoir so that it could be re-sanded.

More birds were landing now, halfway out on the spit.

After inspecting the pump for a few minutes, he shook his head and walked back towards the cottage. The sun was shining on the windows and for a moment...

No! It couldn't be! Anne Marie.

He stumbled frantically up the path and flung open the door. Silence. Stillness. No movement. The vase in the window mockingly resembled a head.

For a while he stood there in a complete daze. What was it he had to do?

Pump. Pump! He sat down slowly on a chair in the sitting room. Of course. The phone. His greasy fingers held the shiny receiver and put an imprint on his ear. George relayed the news to the other end.

"That'll put everything well behind schedule," said the voice, but it remembered to ask, "How are things there, George?"

"Fine," he said, and put down the phone. "Much better."

He sat for some time in the creaky chair, eyeing the duplicitous vase. It was only going to the mirror to remove a speck that he noticed the mark on his ear.

It was lonely without the noise of the sucking, dredging pump. Unnaturally still. But it would be fixed tomorrow. The pulse, the endless throb of the filter beds would resume its habitual hum.

It was five o'clock and slowly getting dark. Time for his last walk round the silent pools. Time to catch the last screeching gulls, the last wisps of light from a fading sky; to watch the bobbing waters as they slipped into darkness; to say goodnight to any of the men still left; to see if the swan had moved nearer to the canal that flowed noiselessly beyond.

But this evening, he walked and walked, circling endless figures of eight round the compact, rectangular lakes.

The wind blew in his face. A breath of memory, of realisation, of emptiness.

It wasn't until darkness finally came that he stooped and looked hard into the deep black, gently lapping waters.

There was nothing left.

Dominic O'Sullivan

After Class

Coming out of the main building, Tanya saw him in the car park, crouching down near the bicycles as if looking for something. It was nice to finish early, she thought, pressing the remote and releasing the automatic lock, its sudden clunking sound making him jump. He stood up quickly, almost guiltily.

"Is everything all right, Jake?" she asked.

He slipped momentarily into the shadows. "Not really, miss."

"Is it your bike?"

Tanya knew full well it was. In the mornings she would often pass him at the bottom of the lane, an invariably windswept figure cycling in from one of the surrounding villages.

"Is there a problem?"

"Knackered," he replied. "Look!"

She could see the vivid slash marks on the bike tyres.

"Who's *done* this, Jake? Do you know who's responsible?"

He shrugged; looked away.

"If you *know*, you *mus*t tell me. Then we can do something about it."

He stared back impassively at her, casting a forlorn figure as he once again knelt down and rubbed his finger over the gaping gash.

"How will you get home?"

He avoided her gaze, content to stare at the immobilised bicycle.

"There should be a bus around half six," he said.

"That's two hours yet. We can't have you hanging round here. Come on, let me take you."

He appeared reluctant to go with her, unwilling perhaps to leave the scene of the crime.

"I've been on one of those buses," she said. "Goes all round the houses, those things?"

He smiled. "People live in houses, don't they?"

There was a slight whiff of schoolboy sweat as he got in the car, placing his jacket on the back seat. It was not unpleasant.

"It's good of you, miss."

"Nonsense. Any of us would have done the same. But if you *do* know, Jake, who's doing this, if you're being bullied, then you *must* come to us straightaway. Okay?"

He nodded. His long legs shifted awkwardly being cramped for space; the front seat was too far forward. She reached over momentarily but then withdrew her hand.

"There's a lever at the side, Jake. You can adjust it. It'll give you more room."

He did as she suggested, shooting unexpectedly into the back seat of the car.

He laughed. "Sorry, miss."

"That's okay. At least you're still in one piece."

"We don't have a car at home."

"I can see."

They were going uphill, passing hedgerows as the lane narrowed, fading light flickering through the branches of trees.

"I hate this corner," she said.

It felt like an intimate confession, revealing the secrets of driving anxieties.

She dropped him at the green. "Which one is it, Jake?"

He pointed to a house on the right where the lights were on in each window.

"Everyone's at home, then," she said.

He got out of the car.

"What about tomorrow? What will you do?"

"I'll be okay. I'll be able to borrow a bike from someone. Thanks for the lift."

She saw him retreating into the darkness as she reversed the car. By the lighted house, he stood for a moment and waved.

For the next two days, Jake was absent. She had already reported the bicycle incident. It wasn't till the following Monday that she saw him again.

When she came towards him, she had the slight sensation that he wanted to back away, to disappear from her; as if the intimacy of car sharing was a distant memory.

"How's it going, Jake?" she asked. "Is it a problem for you getting in?"

"No, miss." He blushed in embarrassment.

"I haven't seen you lately."

"No, miss. I wasn't feeling too good. Had a bit of a cold."

Probably the shock of what happened, she thought. The aftermath.

"How are you getting in now?"

"Same as before," he said. "I got a new tyre."

"That's good," Tanya said. "Let's hope it doesn't happen again. I've asked the caretaker to keep an eye open. Perhaps we should get a CCTV camera in."

"Doesn't work," replied Jake. "We used to have one in the village but they never had enough money to buy a tape. The offy was always getting turned over."

"I think we might do a little better than the village," Tanya replied. "And I think we can run to a tape as well."

"Thanks, miss." he said.

He vanished into a group of other boys. She could hear laughter; she needn't worry. He seemed relaxed, his light brown hair fading into a collection of assorted coloured mops, heads bent down as if devising some kind of conspiracy.

Schools were strange places, she thought. Part detention centre, part nursery, part holiday camp. In the distance, over on the football field, teenage boys in yellow and red tops danced and flickered between the goalposts. The mood was animated, genial and yet someone out there had taken a sharp instrument, a knife most likely, and cut and slashed the tyre. Was it a deliberate, calculated act of vandalism, she wondered , or was it just an opportunistic swipe, the bicycle lying unguarded and vulnerable at the end of the car park?

The term came to an end. Then summer; warmer days, swallows perching on the telegraph wires.

When the long autumn term resumed, with its gradually shortening hours of daylight, she saw a lot more of Jake. The timetable brought them into greater contact, though for most of the time he sat alone at the back of the class, flanked by two empty desks. As she watched and observed him at work with others, occasionally staring out of the long lancet windows with their semblance of Gothic, she noticed he seemed quieter, less animated. He was perfectly amiable with his peers but when the opportunity came to work on his own, he took it.

One Thursday afternoon, she found him alone in the classroom buried in a history book, the others dispatched to the gym or football field.

"No games today?" she asked.

"Verruca," he said. "Have to try not to stand on it. Infectious, apparently, so showers are out."

"That's unfortunate," she said.

"Not really," he replied. "I can't see the point of games anyway. Physical fitness. Most of the others don't have to cycle in each day. That's where *I* get my exercise."

"Yes," she said. There was a pause. "And can you still cycle with your...?"

"Verucca. Oh yes. So long as I don't put any weight on it. I'm sure it'll be fine soon."

She looked up at the clock which dragged itself slowly towards quarter to three.

"You might as well go home, Jake," she said. "No point in staying here. Especially with it getting dark so early."

"Cheers, miss," he said. "Nice one."

It was only when he left the room that she noticed the rectangular spectacle case on the desk where he'd been working. She prised it open and saw the initials J.C.T. inside. What was the C for, she wondered, as she picked up the case and headed towards the car park.

A lone figure was wheeling rhythmically, languidly towards the gate, the last shafts of sun catching on the reflector.

"Jake!" she called, surprised at the sudden loudness of her voice. "Jake!"

But Jake had cycled past the sentry-like shrubs that lined the entrance and was gone.

On leaving the building at around five thirty, Tanya decided to take a detour. It would only add a few minutes on to her journey, she decided. She could drop off the glasses on her way home.

As she passed the flickering clumps of hedges, giant silhouettes in the oncoming darkness, a thought suddenly struck her. She had never seen Jake wear the spectacles, not even briefly, and he had no difficulty deciphering what was on the board. No doubt the glasses were something new, although the case itself looked well worn.

Perhaps it was a vanity thing. Any conspicuous wearing of glasses might single him out as a weakling, diminish his status within the group. And there was, of course, the incident a couple of terms back when someone had vandalised the bike.

At first, she missed the turning, lacking a guide for directions in the front seat, but at the mini-roundabout she turned back and entered the close of council houses where Jake lived. She knocked on the door of the house where she had dropped him. After a few moments, she could hear the sound of shuffling feet from within. The door opened slowly and an elderly woman stared up at her.

"Yes?" she said.

"I'm Tanya Frost. Jake Thompson's teacher. He's left these."

The glass case was held out like some kind of trophy or triumphant object.

"Oh," said the woman. "But he doesn't live here. He's at number twenty three just across the green." She pointed over to the right.

"Oh, I'm so sorry," said Tanya. "I thought this was the house."

As the woman closed the door, Tanya remembered that he had stood outside the house, waving her off. It didn't necessarily mean that he lived there.

When she approached number twenty three, whose sign was scarcely visible from the road, the house was in darkness. Perhaps he wasn't home yet, though she thought she could see a faint light coming from somewhere at the back. She walked round by the cluttered path, opening the small wooden gate that led into the garden.

A light came on in the kitchen window and she saw Jake putting something in the sink. A cup. He looked a forlorn figure as he momentarily bobbed back and forth in front of the uninvited guest. Tanya stretched out a hand and tapped on the pane of glass. She saw him jump for a second then slowly, circumspectly, go towards the door.

"Jake, it's me Tanya," she called, not wanting to alarm him further. She held the glass case up. Her hand alighted on the door handle and it yielded to the touch. She was inside the kitchen now, holding out the case for the second time.

"What is it?" He looked as if he had been asleep, anxious and unsettled now by her intrusion. "Why are you here?" He ignored the object she was waving in her hand, more concerned by her unwarranted presence.

"Are you on your own?" she asked.

"Yes. Why? They don't come in till later."

It was then that the smell hit her, assailed her full force.

"Your glasses," she said, placing them on the ledge by the window.

"Thank you," he said, snatching them immediately and putting them into a drawer. "You didn't need to come. They could have waited."

His body language was hostile. He clearly didn't want her here.

"I thought you might need them."

"I didn't."

"Jake, is something wrong? I mean..."

"Nothing," he said anxiously. "Nothing. Everything's fine."

Tanya looked around her. "Jake, are you here on your own?"

The pile of unwashed dishes, congealed saucepans confirmed neglect, absence...

"You can tell *me*, Jake."

She noticed he was shaking.

"No. Well, it's awkward..."

Tanya remained silent, willing him on to tell her.

"They... kind of left."

"*Left?*"

"Yes."

"*Leaving* you? Here alone?"

"Yes."

"But you're *fourteen*, Jake."

"So?. I can manage. I don't need *them*."

"On your own! What about food?"

"What *about* food?" He laughed a nervous, uneasy laugh. "I can manage."

Her eyes drifted over towards the clutter of crockery groaning in the sink.

"I'm fine without them."

"It doesn't look like it," she said and sat down on one of the wooden chairs. Part of the back was broken.

"We disagreed over something. Had an argument."

"With *both* of them?"

"Yes."

"But why would they leave?"

"Because I *made* them," he said. "Put a stop to it. All the arguments."

She paused a moment for breath.

"Jake. How did you... put a stop to it?"

It was clear from the way he looked at her that he wouldn't answer...wasn't going to answer any more questions.

She didn't see him take the knife from the drawer in which he'd placed the spectacles – sliding it carefully, noiselessly towards him as he reached to turn out the light.

Dominic O'Sullivan

The Ladies' Quarters

"You *are* going to tell them, aren't you?" Helen said after she'd been a few minutes in the office.

Louis shifted a couple of papers uncomfortably from side to side, glanced up at her and said, "Yes. Yes, of course."

"Hmm." Helen was doubtful. "And when will that be?"

"At the appropriate time," came the reply.

He clearly wanted her to go; such questions late in the afternoon! There was a great deal to do, a lot to cover on that gleaming, ordered expanse of desk.

"I see," said Helen and closed the door behind her.

A visitor to Louis's office would have noted the generally forlorn aspect of the room, the paint peeling off the walls and a strange oval damp patch above due to the inconsistencies of the outside drainpipes and guttering. If it was like that in the offices, how much worse would it be in the patients' area, or ladies' quarters, as it was known as? One might also think, however, that the dilapidated state of the administrative buildings would be some kind of sacrificial gesture so that more money could be lavished on the select band of long-term residents. But that would be an optimistic view rather than a realistic one.

As she returned to Block B, Helen switched her concerns from the flaking paint to the word 'appropriate'. *When* was 'appropriate' and for whom?

Her feet made imprints on the soggy grass and she turned to see the lights on in Louis's office, before unlocking the outer gate that led to the ladies' department.

'Appropriate' could be half an hour before the move, even! In these woeful times of trampled on rights, it might even be straightaway, as they did sometimes in companies where employees were asked to immediately clear their desks. Then, flanked by a pair of burly security guards, they would be escorted firmly from the premises – in some cases even helped down the steps!

They could hardly do that with the ladies, of course. Their invariably brittle bones and frail constitution would not permit this. No, they would probably be taken off calmly and at the last minute to their new place of repose. A purpose-built modern unit, perhaps; their final hygienic resting place.

Why did you not tell them? What happened to the courtesy of advance information, she would say to Louis afterwards, if that indeed were the case?

He would defend himself calmly and unflappably. I thought it wise and prudent not to alarm them. They would only become agitated and upset. No, much better to say they were organising an on the spot visit to a new day centre and, as they would naturally find it so much more comfortable and convenient, not to mention light, bright and spacious, it made perfect sense to stay. They would be overwhelmed by the spontaneity of surprise.

It was hard to know with Louis, who was generally more opaque than the previous managers; hard to know what the dictates of his desk were, dictates that floated quietly and anonymously down from on high.

At the reception desk, Jessica appeared half-asleep. To her right, beyond the discarded sweet wrappers, were the TV screens that monitored each of the ladies' rooms.

"Everything okay?" Helen asked. It invariably was. There hadn't been an 'incident' for months. Jessica sprang into a position of suitable alertness.

"And the diet?" Helen pointed to the evidence.

Jessica shrugged. "George, the security guard left a box of After Eights. What could I do?"

Helen smiled. She looked at the notes lying on the desk.

"Elsie's not drinking enough," she commented. "She never does."

"You know, sometimes I wonder if she doesn't do it deliberately."

"Why would she do that?" Helen asked.

"To get more attention. To have more of a fuss made…"

"Hardly," said Helen. "I think there are other considerations."

Jessica glanced over at the clock. "Supper's late," she remarked. "It seems to get later each evening now."

Helen could hear the rattling of the trolley as she went across to her locker. Inside, was her uniform, the pale cream overall. She emerged as an ethereal ghost to drift down corridors.

"Have you heard when they're going to tell them?" she asked.

"How would *I* know?" Jessica replied. No one tells me anything. I'm always the last to know here."

"I just thought you might have heard. I know Louis keeps everything very close to his chest. A whisper, perhaps."

"Maybe some jobs will have to go. What with the new place. Redundancies. That's what Sarah thinks."

"I see," said Helen.

It was unwelcome to have her suspicions confirmed. Another reason for Louis's secrecy.

"I think I'll just make them a cup of tea. They can be having it in the meantime. Till supper comes."

"You're too good to them," Jessica said.

Helen listened to the sighing of the vast, steel urn. Too good. Too good. What did that mean? It was only a cup of tea, for heaven's sake. And in the light of things, the circumstances, of what had been done to these genteel incumbents, the residents, well surely, it was the least they could do!

She put four large cups and two beakers on the poppy-patterned tray, placing it momentarily on the outside table before unlocking the first of the doors.

"Evening, Josie. I brought you a cup of tea."

"Bought?" said Josie. "Did you have to buy it, then?"

"Not bought," said Helen. "*Brought.*"

It was a customary evening exchange. Josie took hold of the mug.

"You girls need to speak clearer. In my day…"

Helen smiled. It was odd, being on the cusp of sixty, and still being referred to as a girl. "I'll take some elly-cution lessons," she grinned. She always said it like that for Josie.

Josie laughed. "You do that," she said. "And tell them it was me who sent you."

With the next four patients, the exchanges were briefer. For two of them, she had to guide the beaker into their hands – skin as thin as paper. Invariably there was a smile, though for Dora tonight there was only confusion and agitation.

"I couldn't find my suitcase," she complained.

"What do you need it for?" Helen asked.

"I couldn't find it."

"Suitcase? Why do you need a suitcase?"

Had she overheard anything? Sensed anything?

The last door was May's. On hearing the door creak open, May put down her magazine.

"How are you, dear?" Helen asked.

"Oh, I'm all right. Bit noisy in the night. Someone was havin' a bad dream."

She pointed to the magazine. "These girls. These single mothers."

"Oh yes."

"It would never have happened when I was a girl. Talking to reporters like this."

"No, I don't think it would," said Helen.

"You'd have been bundled away just like that." She snapped her fingers. "Oh yes. Way away! To a place like this, most likely." She paused for a moment. "It was all wrong. Those men folk got away with it. Blameless as Larry."

"They still do."

"What's that, dear?"

"Get away with it." She held May's hand as she sipped the tea; little birdlike sips.

Each evening, Helen would alternate and go and sit with a different lady. This evening it was May's turn, though if any of the others were asleep or in a 'rumble' as Josie called it, she would generally stay with May. May still did conversations; humour even, at times.

"I don't think I'll go home tonight," she said, taking another sip of tea. "It's a bit chilly."

"We're into autumn now," Helen said.

"Well, there you are. That's another reason. I'd get blown across the garden and probably airborne." She thought for a moment. "Might be fun, though. And I'd be free."

Helen gazed over at her. How would she take the news of a relocation? It was hard to tell. No, she knew May. She wouldn't like it. None of them would. It wasn't much of a place, this damp, gloomy old dump, but it was home. As it had been for so long now.

"Do you like autumn?" she asked Helen suddenly. "Trees turning."

"I do. Yes, I suppose I do."

"Can be slippery, though. All those leaves. I reckon those councils still leave 'em out on the pavements. Lazy buggers, they are. Am I right?"

"Yes, you are, May," replied Helen. She squeezed her hand again. You're always right."

Helen put the key in the lock of her own door later. She didn't like it when they put the clocks back. The long dark evenings and coming back to an empty flat. Her own form of isolation, but in darkness. There was some campaign to stop it, the clock tinkering, that is. Stop all the clocks, she thought. The words seemed oddly familiar; she had heard it somewhere before but couldn't remember where. Yes, they talked about it, the benefits of perennial summertime. Fewer road accidents, more safety and so on, but it never happened. Something to do with Scotland, the Far North, the usual complaints.

At least the inmates didn't have this problem of venturing out, of uncertainty, secured in their own rooms along the corridors of amnesia; of forgetfulness. Amnesia. Yes, that was it. Mislaid and conveniently abandoned. Though there was a visitor sometimes at Christmas, she recalled; an elderly relative, yet Helen couldn't remember whom she came to see. The years had all rolled themselves into one. She would be forgetting herself soon.

A visitor, she thought. A rare visitor! A break of the mould; a link forged with the outside; the far away world outside.

"So near and yet so far," May had said one day. And it had surprised Helen. She said it so calmly and matter of fact.

No, they had not been lucky, the typhoid ladies.

Who was it who used to call them that? She had been reported for it. Gemma, in all probability. Yes, that's who it was. The word had been forcibly deleted and she had, in fact, been given a warning. The adjective, like the ladies themselves, was not permitted to wander into the world outside.

But no, not lucky at all. They were deemed carriers of possible infection and for that they had been isolated, locked up into long, lost years of oblivion. A sentence of incarceration for no crime committed, with no appearance before judge and jury. Succinctly sidelined with no rights of appeal.

She wondered who had been responsible for this; who had sanctioned this lengthy detention of gradual and insidious enfeeblement, of inevitable mental deterioration. As May had said, they had done it with the single mothers, carted them off to the old-style asylums to be out of sight and out of town, while the partners in the deal, the men folk, had been free to carry on, to go about their daily lives, commit yet more girls to institutions, run their businesses, turn in profits, start legitimate families, rearing children within the rules and conditions of wedlock.

And now they couldn't even tell them when they were moving them! There was no redress either. No appeal. Swept away to another place, yet another concealed location. Further out of sight and in no one's mind. For the forgetting, the forgetfulness was both mutual and complicit. The families of the women could forget, too. It was better that way. Easier. There were no complications.

Except there had been one, she thought. Yes, one. Now what was her name? The family had fought. Taken on the system. Fought and fought! They took it to court and won. Brought her back home. A triumph! They had threaded their way through the labyrinth and found a way out for her; a welcome alternative to this lifelong sentence imposed by invisible courts, anonymous clerks and doctors…

She poured herself a drink. She needed it. The prospect of change had made her feel uneasy, restless. The knowing and not knowing. The concealment. The carrying on as normal, as if nothing were going to happen; deceiving and simultaneously betraying...

The TV lulled her to sleep. She wasn't watching it anyway. A group of fatuous people having to escape from a desert island, of having to perform various tasks which included the consuming of unpalatable insects. The other channel was no better; people working at an airport terminal up north. Sleep was the best thing. As if you wanted to watch other people at work when you'd come home from it already. It was the work ethic gone mad!

After prising herself up from the armchair and the flickering telly, she enjoyed a long dreamless sleep. She awoke at eleven. She was on at two. The late shift, the supper shift.

The leaves were turning into congealed soup that clung around her ankles. It was walking among them as she passed through the grounds that the idea slowly came to her.

She could stay, couldn't she at hers? May could. And she would look after her. Yes, get a job in a shop, afternoons weekdays only, just to get a bit of cash rolling in. She'd park May in front of the telly and tell her she'd be back at six. The shops closed around five thirty, as a rule.

"I'm ever so grateful," she could hear May say. "Such a lovely flat and all! Are you sure I'm no trouble?"

"No trouble at all." And she'd kiss her on the forehead and make her a cup of tea.

"It's a good little balcony you've got. What are those flowers?"

"Pelargoniums."

"Lovely colour. Pelargoniums? Didn't they use to call them geraniums?"

"Yes, they did, May, they did."

"Well why did they change the name? What was the point?"

Of course, she'd lose her job once they knew May had gone. Smuggled in the back of Helen's car under a blanket.

"Just lie very still, May. Just while we pass the gate."

"Are you sure it's all right, dear? I feel like stolen goods. I don't want to get you into any trouble."

"Lie still, May. Lie still. It's only a short ride. Freedom is nearer than you think. We'll soon be home."

And May obediently lay down, a pillow plumped against the curve in her back. 'So near and yet so far.'

It would be nice to have company again. Geoffrey had left her nearly nine years ago. And if they found May, found where she was staying, well, she'd refer them to that family that managed the impossible and secured a release. They wouldn't want the publicity from all this, she was sure. And courts were expensive. Lawyers. Slick fibbers in wigs. But what if it was expensive for *her*? What if it went wrong?

No. It had been done before. She would get in touch, make contact with the successful family for advice; how to go about it. She wouldn't be so alone if there was someone on the end of a line she could call.

Two days later, she stepped into the warmth of the building as usual. The other ladies were there, same as they always were, staring into space. One splayed her fingers forward, raising them into the air as if to catch an imaginary mosquito. When she opened the last door, May was not reading as she normally did.

"I feel sleepy today," she said. "Do you think it's the weather?"

Helen wondered when weather had ever permeated this gloomy vault of seclusion.

"I expect it might be. Now, would you like me to make you a nice cup of tea?"

"Please. And have one yourself, won't you?"

"That's good of you."

May smiled.

"I thought we might have a trip out later."

May stared at her disbelievingly. "What about the weather, dear?"

"Don't you worry about that."

"But I'm sleepy today," May repeated. "So sorry, dear."

"You have a rest for a minute. I'll bring you a tea in a moment."

Back of the car, under a blanket, passing through the gates. No one would ever suspect her. Not until…

At eight o'clock, when Jessica was doing the medication, Helen took a walk outside. She needed air; fresh, cool air. The heating was always on and set too high; a subtle means of sedation; something to encourage inertia. From across the way, she could see the lights still on in Louis's office. She would wait for him to leave; to choose her moment.

It was darker than the previous evening. There was no moon. So much the better!

Moving invisibly in the darkness, she would put a note under Louis's door, setting out clearly what she had done, what she had planned, and how, if there was any funny business, she was ready to cause problems, just like that family had done. Jameson! That was it. The name had come back to her. She would check in the files that were gathering dust in the box-room beyond the nursing station.

But then what about the others? Wasn't she singling someone out for preferential treatment? It would be impossible, though, to accommodate them all. There simply wasn't room. And besides, some of them would no longer know where they were. They would still be back in the old place. It wouldn't dawn on them. There'd be no realizing, no recognition.

The light had suddenly gone off in Louis's office, the light which normally glowed brightly late evening across the empty courtyard. He would no longer be sat at his desk, surrounded by wodges of paper and files. She pictured him at the wheel, driving home through the dark narrow lanes.

It was chilly now as she walked to the main building. The smell of antiseptic permeated everywhere but none more so than in the admin block. Everything scrubbed clean as if to underpin perennial standards of unswerving hygiene.

There was a clunk as the swing doors banged behind her. Her footsteps echoed eerily now in the half-lit corridor.

Way up in front of her was Louis's office, the space beneath the door revealing darkness and a convenient gap for mail. She would slide the letter beneath the door, giving it a short, sharp flick so that it flew beyond the door frame and further into the room. If it were half-wedged beneath the door, well anyone could read it.

Suddenly, as she did so, a light came back on in the office. There was a long hollow creak and the door swung open. The billowing shape of Louis was before her.

He saw her bending, stooping, letter in hand.

"Ah, Helen," he said, without any semblance of surprise. "You have a letter for me. That's nice. Do come in, then."

He took the letter out of her trembling hand and smiled.

"It must be urgent at *this* late hour," he added softly, gently closing the door behind her.

Afternoon Tea

"I'm afraid I can't help you," the secretary had said. "It's because…"

"Yes," said James. He knew. Using his best telephone voice, he continued.

"A friend of mine said that he might be living in Downham."

A pause, as if to take in breath. Was she smoking? Surely not. The laws had changed.

"Data protection," the stalling voice said. "I can't give out any information."

There was something, though, in her tone, her reply, which seemed to confirm his 'friend's' hypothesis. He was living in Downham.

"Well, thank you," he said, without a trace of irony. "You've been most helpful."

Confused by the compliment, the voice relented.

"Well, if he ever gets in touch, you know, the reunions they sometimes have, I'll see the message gets passed on."

"Thank you again," said James and put the phone down.

The weather was unusually hot for the time of year and the telephone directory basking in the window felt warm and brittle. The book yielded unwillingly to the touch, as if reluctant to give up its secrets. For a few moments he skimmed the pages to find where it might be. And there it was. How could he have missed it when he looked before? G. J. McBain, All Saints Way, Downham.

Reaching for a pen, he made a note of the address in a small black notebook, along with the telephone number. He wouldn't ring now, not straight away, but instead savour the triumph of his swift success. Besides, he would need to rehearse what to say, and the best telephone voice was something to be used sparingly.

Strange, he thought, how like a confessional the telephone was. The voice speaking into the void, the darkness on the line. And yet it was so easy to detect a lie, with no facial features or beguiling expressions to distract the listener from the truth.

And with Downham, he had scored a hit. The subsequent surprise and hesitation had proved revealing. Data protection had led to data unravelling – data detection!

Pleased with himself, James took a stroll outside. The remains of tomatoes straggled over in pots. Only six weeks ago, the trusses had been laden, but now the wispy strands were all that remained; forlorn clues to a previous bumper harvest, cherry-ripe and sweet tasting.

By the end of the month, he would have made his long-awaited visit; done what was needed, what he felt he had to do.

"I'm an old pupil," he said. "Wharton, James Wharton."

There was a pause.

"Geoffrey's out at the moment." The woman's voice was slightly out of breath. "But I'll make a note of it otherwise I'm likely to forget. When did you say you were coming?"

"I didn't, but I was thinking of the 27th. Would that be convenient?"

"Is that a Wednesday?"

He could hear her rustling some papers; a diary, maybe.

"I believe it is."

"That's a good day. Tuesdays and Thursdays are always out at the moment. I'll mention it to Geoffrey, but if you don't hear anything, then assume it's okay. We're not ones for using the phone much."

"Thank you."

"Well, it's lovely to hear from you."

She was talking to James as if he was an old friend.

"I'm sure he'll be very pleased to see you. There isn't much contact with the old place. Lots of changes. New people, you know."

James wouldn't know either. He wasn't surprised there wasn't much contact with the 'old place'. Who would want to see McBain?

It was a wintry afternoon in December, he remembered. By three o'clock it was almost dark and within an hour they would be free to go. To relieve the drab teaching, the heavy weather made of a 'problem play', McBain had cracked one of his short jokes. James had perhaps been the only one listening, as there was general silence across the room. As the joke stumbled to its stale, predictable outcome, he had involuntarily groaned.

More silence. McBain clenched his teeth; he was no longer smiling.

"Stand up, mister hummer!"

James was taken aback. Normally, there was a collective groan to feeble puns of the McBain variety. This time he was alone.

"Stand up, hummer!" McBain repeated.

James stood up slowly, uncertain.

"Sit down."

McBain was tall and in a couple of strides he was in front of him, lifting him up by his pale sideburns. McBain's hands were large and like rocks. Three swift double blows rained across his face. Their suddenness shocked James and, as he fell backwards, his head banged against the wall. McBain strode back to the front, his thumbs under his jacket lapels.

The smile had returned to his face. Nonchalantly, he referred them back to the text to whichever line they'd been reciting. James didn't hear or follow – not for a long while.

The bus dropped him at the Queen's Arms. It was his best bet, the driver told him.

"It's not far, love." The woman waiting outside pointed him to beyond the garage.

He'd never been to Downham before, unaware of its rural, semi-suburban sprawl. He wondered what sort of house McBain lived in, visualising some kind of austere, three-storeyed Gothic building. He saw himself in its front room delivering his long-prepared speech, not only on the man's brutality but also how he had ruined the only subject he had really loved, reduced to rote teaching in slavish parrot fashion.

James liked those last three words; made a note of them. Slavish, that more or less summed it up. Forty minutes, not just of sporadic terror but total lack of any imaginative freedom or interpretation. They were told! Simply told! How different the discussions at Tech had been, where, even on a Friday afternoon, everyone became animated discussing the likes of Robert Frost, George Macbeth.

All Saints Way was quite different from what he had expected. It was a narrow lane with large reclining bungalows and a small communal green at the end.

He was pressing the doorbell, wondering if it was the kind that worked. Slowly, behind frosted glass, a shape made its way to the door. It swung cautiously open.

"It's James, isn't it?"

"Yes," he replied.

The woman was dark-eyed and diminutive, like an ancient Briton or Celt, he thought; a contrast to the tall, looming frame of her husband. The bungalow smelt of air freshener and disinfectant; he felt his nose start to run.

"When was it you left, James?"

"Twelve years ago."

"Twelve years. Oh. And you waited all that time?"

He had.

"Well, yes," he explained, sensing a minor rebuke. "There was college, university. I moved away."

"University," she said, admiringly. "That's nice. I don't think many of the boys from that school went to university."

Probably couldn't wait to get out of the place, he thought. Almost a life-long aversion to education thanks to...

"Geoffrey retired a couple of years ago," she continued.

Geoffrey? The name sounded almost human.

"Always a difficult thing, retirement."

"I wouldn't know."

"Of course you wouldn't! You're young," she laughed, "You know, they never prepare you for it. I said to Geoffrey he should have gone on a course for it. Not that he would listen." She gave a slight smile.

He probably bullied her too, James thought.

"He'll be pleased to see you, though," she added. "By the way, my name's Frances. Should have said earlier."

"Nice to meet you," said James, conscious of the incongruity of the chronology.

They entered the front room which looked out onto the green. The curtains were half-drawn. Through the gap, he saw a girl limping round with a small bicycle.

"Sunlight's a problem late afternoon. It bothers him. Oh you'll need to speak up. He doesn't hear very well. I suppose he's used to just my voice."

There was something in her tone that spoke of desolation. It sounded like no one came to the house.

"It's James, dear."

McBain was seated in a large upright chair. He turned slowly to one side on hearing her call. He showed no recognition.

"It's….what's your second name, dear?" she asked him.

"Wharton."

"It's James Wharton, dear," she said, raising her voice.

James thought how strange it was hearing his whole name. It made him sound important. Everyone knew him as James. Who was this Wharton?

McBain looked puzzled for a moment, then nodded.

"How many of you were there?" Frances asked. "In your family, I mean."

"Six," said James. "I'm the youngest."

"Six," she repeated. "The youngest one."

McBain gave a faint smile. Frances motioned to James to sit down.

"He doesn't like people standing over him. Makes him feel anxious."

"Yes," said James.

"He gets tired in the afternoons," she said. "On the days he goes to the day centre, he just sleeps all the time. Gives me a break, though."

"I see," said James, unsure. "Would mornings have been better?"

"Not really," Frances replied. "I'll make a cup of tea, shall I?"

"It's okay," James said.

"I'm going to make one anyway. About this time I generally do."

"Thank you," said James.

He was alone with him in the room now, the man almost motionless but smiling back in vague recognition.

"I was your pupil…" James began.

The smile extended a little.

Looking at the smile in the subdued light of the room, James noticed that it was lop-sided. The right side of the face hung down and seemed ever so slightly puffy. A trail of saliva lay just under the chin.

"You don't take sugar?" Frances asked. She was back in the room with tea pot; breezing about.

Sweet enough was what he might have said.

"It was good of you to come." She lowered her voice. "Not been well, you see. Had a…"

She took a handkerchief and wiped his chin.

The drink was strong and welcoming. It offered relief for a time from conversation. They both sipped while McBain watched.

"Nobody else has come," she said. "From the school, that is. No one. Just you."

James nodded.

McBain, seeming smaller now in his high-backed chair, stared back at them.

"Yes, it was lovely of you to come," she said to James, appreciatively.

She said it again when he was on the doorstep, leaving. There was a chill now in the air, he noticed.

"You will come again, won't you?"

Rookery Nook

Slowly, up the long tree-lined drive, came the cavalcade, sauntering at a suitably solemn and reflective pace.

"They're here!" exclaimed Julia to Queen Margarita, who was powdering the royal nose.

"Are they really?" came the reply. "So soon?"

Glancing out of the upstairs window, she saw a procession of around twenty cars gliding towards the building.

"I'm very annoyed with the P.M.," said Margarita," for foisting these ghastly people on me."

"Could madam not have declined?" Julia asked.

"I did everything I could, but then Timothy says there's a big deal hanging on it, some aircraft carrier or something, which would be good for the nation's depressed purse strings, and he thinks that a weekend at the Estate would not only be good P.R. but would obviously help clinch the deal."

"I'm sure he'll be forever indebted to you, ma'am."

"Too bloody right, he will, dear, but then only as long as his political career allows, and these days that's not very long. I mean, look at last year! Two elections in six months! Think of the expense involved not to mention the disruption to the usual TV programmes!"

"I've never understood politics, ma'am."

"Well, if you ask me, it's nothing more than a Public Schoolboy slanging match."

"Does madam not like Public Schools, then? What about the princes? They seem to be enjoying it."

"I'm not particularly bothered either way. It seems to be all games and floggings. Did you know that Rupert was beaten on his *first* day? And by a *prefect*!"

"Was the prefect unaware as to the identity of his victim?"

"I daresay. Though Rupert did say he didn't want to be treated any differently. Well, he certainly realised his wish. In fact, he did seem to get beaten rather a lot in his first year. I did begin to wonder whether he might acquire a taste for it."

"Surely not, madam! He's a prince!"

They were interrupted by a cautious tap on the door.

"The President of Pomonia is here, madam."

"Very well. Tell Watson I'll be down in a minute."

"I think he was hoping you would be downstairs to greet them."

"It is *not* his business to hope. They should consider themselves damned lucky that I'm doing this bloody thing in the first place!"

There was a chastened 'Yes, ma'am' from the other side of the door.

It was while Margarita was getting ready that the telephone rang. The special phone! Julia went to answer it.

"Yes, it is, but madam is very busy," Margarita heard her say. "She is entertaining the Pres..."

"Very urgent!" said the voice at the other end and in a French accent. "Très urgent, s'il vous plaît!"

"What is it, Julia?" asked Margarita.

"It's a man with very bad English," came the reply. "Said his name was Disco or something."

"Could it be Piscard?"

"Very likely, madam."

Margarita picked up the receiver. A panic-stricken voice could be heard from the other end.

"What a surprise!" Margarita said. "But it's not my birthday. At least, not the first one."

"Non, non," said the invisible voice. "It is très urgent."

For several minutes, the room fell silent. Julia could hear the sound of Margarita drumming her fingers on the table and the noise of furniture being moved downstairs.

"They've parked under the tree," Julia said, but Margarita was still listening intently on the phone.

At length, she replaced the receiver and sat down briefly.

"Well, well!" she muttered.

"Is everything all right, madam?"

It clearly wasn't.

"That, my dear, was the French President."

Julia glanced up. Margarita always used the words 'my dear' when a problem was afoot.

"He tells me he had to put up with that odious couple all weekend as they wanted to stop off in Paris on the way here and that during the banquets given in their honour, they were stealing most of the cutlery and even the carving knives!"

"Good heavens, madam!"

"No doubt souvenirs to give their grandchildren or to show off to the humble citizens of Pomonia."

"I've never liked that name," commented Julia.

"Me neither. It sounds like some kind of lavatory cleaner. Oh well, it can't be helped. Someone has to live there. Let's count ourselves lucky *we* don't have to." She looked briefly at the carriage-clock. "I suppose we should be going downstairs."

"Will the children be dining, too?"

"I very much doubt it. There are some things you *simply cannot* expose children to. Besides, they shot off when I mentioned our visitor's name."

"Rupert included?"

"Yes. He's gone off on a fishing weekend with his old prefect. They're the best of friends now, apparently."

"What about the cutlery problem?"

"I've already thought about that."

For that particular moment, Margarita declined to say more. As they descended the staircase, both Julia and Margarita could see the flotilla of cars parked under the two plane trees.

"How silly!" exclaimed Margarita. "Did no one tell them?"

"Apparently not, ma'am."

"Typical lack of organisation, don't you think? Have a word with them after, won't you?"

"Of course, madam."

Margarita entered the banqueting room to the obsequious smile of her elected Prime Minister. It's all very well for you to grin like a Cheshire cat, she thought. At least you can bugger off at the end of the evening whereas I'm stuck with them all in my own home. She had a good mind to tell him what Piscard had said about the cutlery. The warning. That would certainly wipe the smirk off his face!

"May I introduce, ma'am, the President of..."

Margarita glanced in the direction where the oily palm was indicating.

Rupert had squeezed it once in a fit of enthusiasm and had recounted the tale on several occasions. "It was like a soggy bath sponge, mummy," he'd complained. "Damp and clammy."

She shuddered for a moment and looked again at the offending, guiding hand.

"But there's no one there," she almost said. And then, of course, she had the manners and propriety to glance down and there, indeed, was the object of her search.

For a moment, she nearly gasped. Standing next to the Prime Minister, who in moments of vexation was often referred to as the 'short arse', was an even tinier man. He made the P.M appear briefly as a giant. Perhaps that was why he had invited him as political guile knew no bounds. Such a dramatic contrast could only improve the P.M's standing.

Graciously, she nodded down to the diminutive President and felt a sharp twinge in her neck. Perhaps it would be better when everybody was sitting down.

The President smiled a shifty, toothy smile but Margarita was still thinking about the cutlery and her favourite quotation from Noel Coward.

"Never trust a man with short legs," it began. Now how did it finish? Annoyingly, it eluded her as they proceeded towards the banqueting table. Margarita cast a glance at the selection of food. It was suitably impressive and, commendably, the emphasis was on local produce. In years to come they were to use the word 'sourced' during her long reign, which would invariably set her teeth on edge, but for the moment everything was 'source-free.'

"Don't forget," she said to the lady Julia, "to have a word with them."

"I'll do it at once, madam," she replied and left the room.

In the more subdued lighting of the hall, three men in strange-looking suits were sprawled across some of the reception chairs. They stood up when she approached, a touch anxiously and ominously, she thought.

"It's to do with the cars," she announced to the burliest one, who looked as if he was in charge.

He stared back blankly at her.

"The position, you see. There is a problem."

Again he gazed at her uncomprehendingly but then immediately one of the men made towards the staircase and said something.

"No, no," said Julia. "Not *your* position. It's to do with the vehicles."

The second man had not understood either. "No speak English," he said, turning the last word into three syllables. Within a minute, he returned with a slightly slimmer, wiry-looking colleague.

The President's retinue must be vast, she thought. All *these* people!

"Good day," said the wiry colleague, stretching out a hand.

Julia explained the situation and the delicate problem with the trees. He listened carefully, nodding from time to time.

"So, you see, you'll have to move the cars."

The man inclined his head, sparrow-like and said, "Thanking you, but so sorry. Not possible. President choose spot. We cannot change."

"But the thing is..."

"Thanking you, but it is impossible to say no to President."

For a moment, he appeared forlorn, crestfallen.

At least I tried, thought Julia. At least I...

"They won't hear of it," she said to Margarita later.

But Margarita had drunk one glass too many and had forgotten what it was all about.

"Get yourself a drink, luvvy," she said to Julia, motioning to a hovering footman.

Oh dear, thought Julia. She hoped that madam wasn't in the mood for singing Irish sea-shanties, which she sometimes did when she was in festive spirits.

"Go on, Jools," repeated Margarita encouragingly.

Julia noticed that three or four cushions had tactfully been placed on the President's chair so that at table he was not conspicuously lower than any of the neighbouring guests. Opposite Margarita sat the President's wife, an eminent and distinguished scientist by all accounts, who lugubriously dribbled her soup. She was the last to finish, but as she did so, the soup bowl and accompanying cutlery were instantly whisked away.

"Very nice soup," remarked Julia, but Mrs. President only looked blank and nodded slightly sourly.

"Is it normal," one of the officials was asking through the interpreter, "for her Majesty's handmaiden to sit with us at table?"

Julia realised that the enquiry was directed at her. 'Handmaiden'. She quite liked the term whereas 'equerry' always reminded her of a horse.

"Her Majesty likes to think in terms of a bicycle monarchy, rather like in Holland," came the reply.

"It is good for the health, I suppose," the official responded.

After the peach sorbet came the speeches during which Julia thought she could detect Margarita nodding off. She was familiar with those wilting eyelids, the semi-glazed expression which betokened torpor.

"I've had enough," said Margarita.

Julia thought she was referring to her alcohol intake.

"After Short-Arse has said his bit, I'm off to bed." She burped discreetly. "At eleven o'clock there's Brain of Britain on the radio."

"Madam, you can't!"

"Just try and stop me!"

The Prime Minister was addressing the President and his eminent scientist wife. Both bowed graciously. Margarita stifled a yawn.

"Who writes this rubbish?" she said to Julia in a slightly louder than usual enquiry.

A couple of heads turned.

It was in the early hours of the morning that Julia heard the familiar cawing sound. From the far side of the park, they sounded gently evocative and reassuring. It was when they perched closer to the building that they sounded less melodic. Listening for a moment to their abrupt, staccato cries, she fell promptly back to sleep.

Shortly after ten o'clock, the President suddenly announced that he wanted to take a drive around the estate. Sweeping out with his vast retinue behind him, he stepped towards the favoured limousine. Suddenly there was an audible gasp from members of the manicured assembly. For a moment, in the dappled sunlight, the pock-marked vehicle looked as if it was riddled with bullet-holes. As Julia glanced upwards and at the suspended branches of aerial twigs, she realised what had happened.

The President unleashed a volley of clearly unrepeatable language, to which a number of aides appeared shamefaced. The precariously overhanging nests with their bulky incumbents had had a successful morning. The once resplendent limousine was peppered with streaks of birdlime. Margarita, on hearing animated cries, had ventured downstairs now, yet on seeing the transformed limo, all she could do was laugh.

The President and his scientist wife glared back venomously. This was followed by further ranting at the hapless officials, while someone ran for buckets of warm water.

"The President is leaving at once!" the shaky translator informed them. "It is a great insult to us!"

"I thought you'd told them," said Margarita, nudging Julia, after he'd left them.

"I did, madam, but they took no notice. They gave the impression it was a hallowed spot and declined to move."

"I suppose it must seem rather discourteous," Margarita replied. "My husband Georgie always wanted me to have the tree pruned or even chopped down but I'm so glad I didn't!"

They watched from the window as the frantically cleaned car was preparing for imminent departure.

"But, I admit, it's not every day that deities get shat on," Margarita continued.

Julia was wondering whether to adopt her suitably shocked pose, though with the passage of time in the household it was beginning to lack conviction, when suddenly there were more hurried footsteps outside. She opened the door to a breathless cook.

"Madam," he said, staring past Julia and in the direction of Margarita, who had now sat down. "All the breakfast spoons have gone!"

Blazing a Trail

We go together as a unit; a family outing, a social event. Dad puts his cap on and scarf. Never goes anywhere without it, no matter what the weather. "I never get colds, you see, son." Even so, it's a bit bizarre in the summer when you're sitting on a beach. Not that we go to the beach or…

One day, he realised at the bus stop, he hadn't got it on – his cap, that is. Dashed all the way back for it. Mrs. Wilmslow from the corner shop – she was waiting for a bus, too – said he looked quite becoming. Always fancied a man with a bald head.

"Don't say that to him," I said. "That word!"

"Which word's that, dear?" she asked.

"Bald," I said. "He has a thing about it."

Under his arm is a newspaper. He holds it like a cricket bat as if he's going out to bat; to gladiate in the middle. He used to play, but not now. Knees and back. Sporting injury. Refers to it when asked.

Harry's there, too. Dad's brother. And Ronnie and Jonathan.

Jonathan looks in the mirror, as he always does. A parting look to see he's still there. Still as good-looking as yesterday. He fiddles with his hair while Harry sucks a mint. Usually a Murray Mint. No hurry.

We step out onto the landing. A grey floor, a grey day. The door shuts with its harsh, unwelcoming slam. Some slams are better than others but not this one. And it seems to get worse.

We have to get the lift down – knees, of course. Sometimes me and Jonathan walk the stairs and wait, where it takes an age. Harry got stuck in it once – nearly an hour.

"What did you do?" we said.

"I read the paper," he said.

"No, to get out?"

"Just waited," he said.

There's a whirr as it creaks its way up and, hesitantly, as if waiting for a tip, the doors open. There's a smell of stale ketchup, spilt from a thousand takeaways, of greasy chips and beer. But Harry, with the perpetual mint, won't smell it. He's impervious.

Marcia is still written over the walls, achieving immortality as her name bobs, rides up and down in the lift all day. Nobody gets on in our journey. No one. No one's going anywhere today, except us. It's our day.

As we cross the square, I notice that someone's put detergent in the fountain again. It comes billowing across the open square to meet us. Mobile soap suds blowing in the wind.

"Silly bleeders!" says Harry. "They should have used it on themselves. Some of them have never had a wash!"

His cheek is bulging with a mint so, for a moment, and in those wide glasses, he looks like a giant goldfish. A goldfish with a mission, however. As we *all* have. It's our day.

Harry says something else but Jonathan's not listening. He's looking at his fleeting reflection in a row of shop windows. We're on the far side of the square now. Jon looks at his watch. We're on time. No reflection there, though, mate.

We cut through the park. In the evening, when it's closed, it adds half a mile to the journey, unless you jump the railings, though that's beyond Dad's and Harry's capability. It's always damp here and the leaves are slippery. Harry wants to take my arm – I can see it – but he's too embarrassed to. One day, he'll have to, unless he steps into much awaited retirement. He goes skating from side to side as if he's on ice. Maybe a broken leg's easier to overcome than holding onto a nephew's arm.

And Ronnie is silent, as always. Never speaks outside. It's as if the plants and trees hold hidden microphones – he probably thinks his thoughts are recorded, too.

The park is over. Harry stops zigzagging about and we cross the main road.

And there behind, the Rose and Crown – the sweet rose of temptation – even for me now, adult, eighteen and legal – is where we're at; where we're heading. Puddles in the uneven tarmac, permanent puddles that hardly ever dry out. You could keep carp in them, I'm told. Silent and deep.

Not much of a queue today. When the other office was relocating, we used to be 'monthlies' and the place was chocker. Now it's every two weeks. Much quieter.

Dad and Harry shuffle forwards; me, Ronnie and Jonathan behind. Jonathan's wondering if there's anyone looking at him but there's only an old man in the corner and he's fast asleep.

The clock is ten past eleven. We sign each of us in turn. But when Harry goes to inscribe his promising signature, they hand him a piece of paper.

"Your new signing time, Mr. Norton."

What's this? And dad, too? All of us? All different times?

"Yours is a Tuesday, Mr. Norton." That's dad.

I don't advise it. They don't know about Ronnie. They can't change his time. No. He'll burn down the office, I know he will. I want to tell them about it, about what might happen but she'll say I'm being threatening – call security!

I remonstrate with them, the counter people, on behalf of all of them. Of dad and Harry and Ronnie – even Jonathan.

It'll do Ronnie's head in. It's all or nothing! Please, please, don't split us up! We have the same name, the same time!

"We're relocating our interviews and appointments."

So which is this? A quick exchange over the counter! No, we go together!

The charred remains of the office stand forlornly behind the Rose and Crown now. The police don't seem to know who did it. I could have told them except, of course, I wouldn't. It's the last thing I'd want to do. I tried to warn them – sort of. And they should have known I had good reason for doing so, for arguing, persuading, trying to change their minds. Don't change it. Don't change us. Leave it…!

The new office is a bit further across town. We have to go by bus. Harry's legs! But we're all the same time again, so, if you like, Ronnie's done us proud.

Only just keep it as it is. Don't change it. We go together. It's our day out. Things are fine. We're happy as we are!

A Drop of Sun Tan Oil

"This is Alex" said Joe.

I nod as Alice stretches out a hand.

He said he was bringing someone, meeting someone but I didn't know it was *this* kind of someone.

Alice's hand is frail and flimsy. It flutters like a moth as I relinquish it. She is tall and blonde; healthy looking. Scandinavian even, although the only Scandinavians I've ever met are brown haired sailors that frequent the pubs on the Hoe.

Their body language says it all. The proximity of intimacy.

"And what do you do?" asks Alice.

"Not a lot," I say.

Damn it, I think afterwards. My being unforthcoming will perhaps give too much away.

"I only work three days a week," I add, feeling a slight guilty twinge.

"Sounds very nice." She smiles. "I wish I did the same."

"Alex has never been a work devotee," explains Joe. "Bit of a lazy arse, really."

"I'm sure he isn't." Alice smiles again.

I can't dislike her. She's engaging and pleasant and unlike Joe's last girlfriend, she has a good line in conversation.

"You still haven't said," says Alice.

"Said what?"

"What it is you do."

"Oh, that!"

"Yes, that."

"That's 'cos he can't remember," says Joe. "It's because he's a lazy bum."

"Stop being so rude," says Alice. She taps him on the chest, hairs just visible above the T-shirt line. It's as if she's asking some unruly child to be quiet.

Banter. I suppose that's what it is. Joe shows our intimacy by insults and jibes.

"Translations," I say.

"Pardon?"

"Translations. That's what I do."

"Oh."

"The lazy plonker's half-Spanish."

"Ah."

Alice makes encouraging little noises, as if each 'oh' and 'ah' will lead to more extensions of conversation, more information and more revelations.

"It's probably why he's lazy. Mañana, mañana. You..."

"Stop being so racist, Joe!"

She's got her school teacher's hat on. Racist? I can't see what's racist.

"I'm not racist," protests Joe, echoing my thoughts. "It's just the Mediterranean lifestyle. You know, the laid-back approach."

I don't know why she's defending me. I can cope. Besides, I like Joe abusing me. I like the attention. It makes him seem leaner, more angular.

And at the reminder of my Latin connections, I think of the time we went to Bilbao, through Spain, and then on to Galicia where it rained all the time. After three days of rain, I was annoyed with Galicia. Joe's shorts were confined to the suitcase; he wore clothing more suitable for the cooler, rainy climate.

"I wish I could speak foreign languages," says Alice. "How many do you speak?"

"We'll have to take his word that his Spanish is okay," replies Joe. "He's pretty incoherent in English, though."

Alice doesn't tap him this time but turns her back on him, dismissive and disdainful.

"You must be very clever to know them."

"No," I protest. "Anyone can."

"Do you speak any others?"

"French, Italian. Some Russian..."

"Russian!" She's impressed.

"That's when he was going through his communist period. Dostoyevsky and all that."

Joe pronounces it like Dusty Effsky.

"Dostoyevsky was before Communism," I reply.

Abuse, I can take but inaccuracies... well, that's something else.

"It's all Commy," says Joe.

Joe seems slightly startled with that 'worm's turned' look. I suppose I'm forgetting myself by answering back. Get back to the insults, that way we're on an even keel.

"She likes you," Joe confided to me a couple of weeks later.

"She's got good taste."

He's smiling, annoyingly, at me.

"You don't mean...?"

"Oh no. No. She's not after your body. She's got me to contend with for that. No, it's your mind."

"You're winding me up."

"You can ask her."

"As if!"

He spits out the cherry stone that was protruding in his cheek. A little semicircle of discarded husks is forming on the ground.

"Alice wants to go to Cornwall for the weekend."

"Doesn't she know better?" is my reply.

I should explain that as Devon lads we see very little merit in Cornwall.

"Where will you go?"

"Coast walking."

"Is she up for that?"

I have a vision of us in Spain, hill climbing, the sun beating down on Joe's bronzed back. His hair was lighter too, bleached by the sun. At the end of each day, he would ask me to put the sun-tan cream on. 'After Sun' the label said. I would work it in slowly, methodically, using the tips of my fingers as if I were a trainee washing someone's hair or applying some kind of massage. And as I did so, my cock would stiffen, and depending on what I wore, forming a tent-like construction within my underpants. Thankfully, Joe had his back to me, otherwise I would have been exposed to ridicule, to taunts.

Uncle Alf once told me that human beings had had tails, way back.

"Was that before or after nipples?" I asked him.

The same historian had also told me of male breastfeeding, one afternoon when we were clearing out the garden shed.

If we had tails, I thought, our feelings would be so naked, so exposed, so clear to see. Thumping away like some exuberant Labrador after a mere two-hour absence.

On the day before the rains, Joe had asked me to put some lotion on his chest.

"*You* can do that," I nearly said. Nearly, but my surprise circumvented words.

This, of course, would have been far more dangerous, would easily have given the game away, had I not had the foresight to slip my shirt outside my shorts. I applied the cream slowly while Joe closed his eyes. I started with the tops of his shoulders – peaches turning to olive brown.

It was when I went lower down, to the soft taper of hair that extended upwards from his belly button, that I knew I was leaking heavily.

The sod, I thought. The bloody sod!

I looked for signs of reciprocation, of appreciation, but everything was tantalisingly vague. I turned away from the finished product – Joe smelling now of palm trees and coconut.

When he fell asleep that night in the adjoining bed, I tiptoed to the cold ceramic tiles of the bathroom to put an end to the pain and misery – 'blue balls' as my friend Ronnie once described it.

They both went off for the weekend to Cornwall, had one fine evening when they got there and then the rest was sea-mist and rain.

"Not much walking, then?"

"Not enough," said Joe.

"I suppose time for other things," I smiled sleazily, adding emphasis to the self-evident.

"You *must* be joking! Alice suggests these youth hostels and then they boot you out at ten in the morning. It was too damp to do anything else outdoors."

I envisage them on a crag, a bend in the coast, the cliffs. Purple heather and gorse with an attendant bumble- bee. There's a haze on the horizon; the sun is mild, the wind gentle and reassuring. I sense Joe's frustration and feel sorry for him.

If I were in his shoes, I suppose. Size elevens instead of eights.

Two weeks later, Joe has an amended plan.

"South Hams," he says.

"That's more like it," I say, advocating parochialism.

"We'll take a couple of tents."

"A couple!"

"She wants *you* to come."

"No," I say. "Who on earth wants a gooseberry?"

"*She* does."

"No," I protest again and re-invoke the fruit.

"You're getting a little prickly," Joe says with a half-smile. "Would you like it from the horse's mouth?"

He's calling Alice a horse.

"Joe said you'd come," she says in the pub later.

I nearly choke on my beer.

"I've got to revise," I say.

"What bollocks!" Joe replies.

"It would be nice if you could," says Alice.

She has all the powers of persuasion that Joe lacks. The sensitivity, the subtlety. It's impossible for me to say 'no' now.

Bugger them, I think. I'm caught up in this weekend that I don't want. Me alone and wanking in my bed while their royal cubicle is expanding splendidly and rocking at the sides.

"We'll drive down Friday evening," Alice suggests. Alice has something neither of us has. Alice has a car.

"Sounds fine," I say in a helpless sort of way.

The weather's set fair and we head for Joe's favourite cove. The countryside is white and green. Lanes full of cow parsley and hawthorn with its heady smell of fresh mown grass. They pull the roof back and the sun catches Alice's hair. They're well prepared. Beer and sandwiches on the beach. Everything tastes better out in the open air and in his exuberance Joe wants to fling a bottle out to sea.

"You moron!" Alice chides. "There's enough rubbish out there without you adding more."

She has a sense of responsibility, a reluctance to violate nature.

"What if there's a message in it?"

"In what?"

"A message of undying love."

She thinks he's laughing at her and Joe breaks into song.

"Message in a bot-tle," he intones and blows into the neck. It makes a booming sound. Like a bittern, I'm told, though I've yet to see one.

We put the tents up in the moonlight. It's not easy.

"Tomorrow night," says Alice, "we'll put the tents up first and then get pissed."

"Whatever," says Joe, who doesn't care.

It's the first time I've heard Alice say anything remotely vulgar. Joe's corrupting her, I think to myself. The animal within is despoiling beauty, but then that doesn't fit either, for in the shafts of moonlight Joe looks different too – more lean and angular and yet more striking.

The next day we walk. Catch a ferry. We stop off at a pub. The tent on the back has turned me into a snail. Only Alice, the driver, is unburdened. She puts a hand into Joe's back pocket; the rest of him is concealed by tent and rucksack. And talking of tents...

"How much further?" complains Alice.

She takes the words right out of my mouth, but if *I* had said them, I would have been called a wimp, a wuss, whatever...

"One more hill," promises Joe. "And then it's on the other side of the ridge."

We look disbelievingly but Joe is resolute. And as we round the corner, Joe's true to his word.

"Shit!" he exclaims. "Grockles!"

I explain to Alice what a grockle is.

We sit on the beach in the flanking symmetry of beer bellies. I wonder if Joe will ever get one – the hair tapering from the belly button in Spain.

They both swim out in the choppy waters. I sit with my book and occasionally look out to sea. Gradually, the visitors are going. The beach will soon be ours. Joe opens another bottle, pours Alice and myself a drink.

"We'll put the tent up," she insists.

Joe is reticent but Alice has decided. In record-quick time and with no hiccups both tents lie on a sandy mound above the beach.

"Will it be safe from the tide?" she asks.

"Trust me," says Joe and smiles.

During the preparations, one glass of beer has capsized.

"That'll be yours, Joe," says Alice.

"Shit!" says Joe. "What a waste!"

He goes back to the car; returns with fresh supplies.

Alice talks about a career change as the light starts to fade. She's fed up with being Miss Nobody, the secretary. She wants to go into nursing. I can picture her in a nurse's uniform – she'd be quite good, I think.

"Male orthopaedic," she says. "That's what I want."

"What's wrong with the women?" Joe asks.

"All bedpans and enemas," she says. "Besides, everyone wants the boys."

"Do they?" I ask.

"They're all quite young," she carries on. "Motor bike accidents. It'll be quite fun."

I look across at Joe but he stares back disapprovingly. Alice takes no notice and continues her enthusiasm.

It's only during my second bottle of beer that I realise Alice is quite drunk. Her speech volume's gone up a bit and she laughs more readily. Joe offers me another beer but I haven't finished the first one yet. He pours it into his glass and chinks spontaneously with Alice.

It's nice, I think. Nice of them to ask me. To make me feel...

I look out again to sea in the fading light. Alice is still laughing and they talk together a while longer. I go for a walk along the beach, leaving them in each other's company, watching the slowly appearing stars.

When I return it's quiet. Alice lies sleeping on the sand; the bottles of beer behind her like a collection of fallen trophies.

"Such a beautiful night," I say softly. But there's no acknowledgement, no reply.

I turn towards Joe who also lies comatose against a rock. Nothing will disturb them it seems; the sleeping lovers. I glance at some of the empty bottles of beer and notice that Alice has drunk most of the stronger ones. No wonder she's out like a light. Her occasional snores and grunts contrast with a gentle lapping of the waves.

I look back towards Joe, to the neat proportions of his neck and shoulders, his long, hairy and slender legs. My eyes are stealing glances; taking him all in; taking the liberties of gazing at him in a way I couldn't have done in the exposed light of day.

And like the moon, I'm rising – slowly, gently up.

I look at his pale maroon shorts, the line of skin between shirt and pants. It is lean and muscular with not an ounce of excess fat.

I am moving closer to him now while Alice snores. And I lean forward and kiss him silently on the mouth, to which he might wave his arms for a moment, as if dismissing a persistent fly.

And now I gaze back down towards his crotch and then...

I don't know why I'm doing this. I shouldn't, but I reach forward to undo the top button; slowly slide down the dormant zip.

Alice snores on, varying her sound a little.

Joe is semi-erect as I go down on him. Immediately, it seems, he stiffens, rising to maximum length. I make sure to keep him well within me, but believe me, it's not easy. He moves a little, as if wanting to turn on his side. I steal an upward glance but thankfully his eyes are firmly shut and so I carry on. I feel a rush within him, which is also me; he gives a sudden sigh.

Quickly I withdraw from him like a thief in the night. By pulling up the zip, I am making good my escape. But as for the top button, it's too risky to do it up, so I shall leave it as it is, open and tantalising.

I move to the edge of the sandy mound where we've pitched camp and behind is the flap of the tent. Joe's essence is with me. I hold on for as long as I can, then gently swallow.

For a long time I sit looking out to sea, then finally creep into my abode, the solitary uninhabited tent. Will they be okay under the stars, I wonder? Should I go back and wake them? What if it gets cold?

It doesn't. It's warm and humid inside the tent and outside too. I listen to the sound of the waves breaking against the shore. Rhythmic; endless.

When I awake next morning, they're both breakfasting. Joe is without his shirt in the warm sun and immediately on seeing him I feel a stab of guilt.

"What time do you call this?" he says a touch sarcastically. Our eyes meet but there's no rebuke there.

"Alice has already been into the village for some milk."

"Oh. Right. Thanks."

I'm pouring cereal into my bowl. Alice is well organised; she's thought of everything.

"How are you both?" I ask.

"Fine," says Alice.

"Why shouldn't we be?" questions Joe.

"It's only you both crashed out on the beach last night. I didn't know whether to wake you."

"Excellent sleep, man," says Joe. "Under the stars. And dreams."

"I can't hold my drink," apologises Alice.

"She can't," confirms Joe.

"And I was tired," she says.

"Yes. That too."

For the rest of the day we walk together along the coast. They've both made sandwiches and we picnic up on the cliff. Joe is in buoyant mood. He talks more than usual today. When I look at him and my eyes stray towards his crotch, I feel guilty and a little ashamed. I took advantage and I seized an opportune moment in a highly underhand way. But I feel closer too somehow and a little self-conscious. I wonder if it'll wear off, the latter.

Alice drives us back home and I'm left alone in my flat. I'm not sure what their plans are. Alice has to work tomorrow; has an early start.

I don't see Joe for three or four days. Subconsciously, I've been avoiding him — self-imposed exile is the price for my transgression.

But on Friday he drops by on the way home from work.

"Next weekend," he says. "We're doing the next bit of coast."

"Should be nice," I say. "Have a good time."

He stops, slightly surprised, and looks at me. "You'll be coming, won't you?"

"No. I've got some things to do in the flat."

"Such as?"

He has me stumped. I can't think of anything. In vain, I try to think of chores I have to do; tedious chores.

"You won't want me around. Cramping your style. You and Alice."

He looks directly at me. "Yes, we do, mate."

His concern is genuine. "Me and Alice."

"Well, I..."

"We'll pick you up at six, then."

I feel a simultaneous wave of gratitude and relief.

He turns to go but just as I'm about to close the door, he turns back for a moment and looks at me.

"Oh yes," he says. "Last time. You know, at the cove.."

I think I know what's coming.

"I opened my eyes, just for a second, and..."

I stare down at the floor, down at size eleven feet.

"I'm sorry, mate," I say. "I shouldn't. It was all..."

He smiles, appears unconcerned, puts a hand on my shoulder.

"It's just..."

"Don't worry," he says. "Alice can't hold her drink."

"So she said."

"And so she's always likely to pass out."

"Oh."

"It'll happen again, I'm sure."

"Yes."

"And...it can get boring being on your own."

I don't know what to say. I murmur goodbye and the door shuts with a resounding click.

I can't say no.

And once again, I can see myself standing behind him, rubbing sun-tan oil across his back and shoulders, staying in some poky little hotel out in the wilds of Spain.

Wind

At ten thirty she was woken up by the telephone; a call summoning her to the downstairs sitting room. She had been dozing, in all likelihood; a dreamless doze when the noise had cut in.

Elspeth moved circumspectly down the stairs. It had happened once before when, half-asleep, she nearly tumbled and fell at the curve in the staircase. And when she'd picked up the phone, it was a stupid, rasping voice telling her she'd won a prize! A prize! At this hour! And how could she have *won* when she hadn't even entered anything?

But now she trod carefully, switching on the light which flickered and fused. In the accompanying darkness, she managed to locate the receiver and pick it up.

"Mrs. Hamilton?" said the voice.

"Speaking?" Speaking but listening.

"I'm sorry to tell you..."

Words chopped up. The main message.

"Mr. Hamilton... he passed away... around ten o'clock."

'Passed away' - not the 'd' word, she thought. She wouldn't have minded the 'd' word, but then 'passed away' didn't sound too bad either.

She pictured Henry travelling on some road somewhere, late at night, looking with difficulty at the road signs. Travelling. Travelling.

"Are you okay, Mrs. Hamilton?" She was being asked a question.

Okay. Yes, okay. What should she say?

"Yes, yes," she said. There was a pause. "Thank you for telling me."

"You're welcome," said the voice.

Welcome. It sounded oddly impersonal, as if she'd been querying some payment with the gas board.

Elspeth put the phone down and turned on another light. The room stared back at her, poorly-lit, unconsoling. Automatically, she went into the kitchen and made a cup of tea. She switched the radio on. It was her favourite newsreader; voice mellow like plums – soft and fruity.

Perhaps she *should* have been there. Sitting beside him. But then they'd told her to go home, hadn't they? It was what *they* thought best. She was tired, in need of sleep. They would ring her.

For eight weeks, ever since it happened, she'd journeyed twice a day to the hospital. The weeks took on a steady routine. She even got to know some of the bus drivers, though on some routes there were no conductors with whom she could have a chat. And on the meandering route of the 41, there were plenty of conductors who liked a bit of a natter. There was one who sang in the evenings, until he was told off, apparently. Lengthy Scottish ballads. Somebody had complained, no doubt, to the Transport Board.

"No songs tonight, Archie?"

Archie put his fingers to his lips. "I'm not allowed."

"That's the entertainment gone, then," she replied. "I suppose you could always take up juggling."

"Aye, I could," said Archie, "Except I'm a bit of a butterfingers."

The word had made her laugh as she pictured it. Archie trying to catch something and the way he said 'butterfingers'. It was like some kind of intimate confession.

She liked his eyebrows. They were dark and expressive. No wonder he wanted to sing on the platform of a double-decker bus!

She lifted the mug to her lips. The tea brought her back to reality, to the stillness of the room and the slightly sombre, sour-smelling furniture. The least comfortable chair was to her left and she sat in it bolt upright.

It was too late to phone people, she thought. Inconsiderate to, anyway. She pictured them lying beneath the covers, partners, partnered, the soft swish of sheets masking the news that was to come from 5, Wilburton Terrace.

It was something for her to do in the morning. Another sip. The tea tasted weaker now.

And now, at a stroke, her routine was washed away. The twice daily visits, the occasional serenade by Archie. The long corridors, the dark evenings, making her way through the hospital grounds.

She slept for longer than she intended. The morning news programme on the radio was nearly at an end. A late breakfast felt like a transgression because she should be down there, down...

And then she remembered. There was no one in the hospital now. Nobody to visit. The side-room in which Henry was stationed, consisting of six beds had offered little in the way of conversation. It was a sleeping room. God's waiting room...

And when she'd visited Polly, her neighbour, two years back, who'd been found on the front path, the hospital had an identical six-bed waiting room with five other ladies all sitting by their beds while Polly slept. The ladies had had more to say than the men. The lady with the shock of hair, sitting in the middle, was called Vi.

During a lapse in conversation, when a blanket of silence had unfurled over the ward, Vi had suddenly remarked "There's somebody up there..." She jerked a finger towards the ceiling, "...havin' a bloody good laugh."

Elspeth smiled and nodded, though it was not a smile to be reciprocated. Vi's face was the aspect of stone. She turned back to the sleeping Polly.

But now, she was no longer constrained to a timetable. She could go out when she liked, do what she wanted. It was a strange, peculiar feeling. The day stretched out like a vast, uncharted sea – and she, a rudderless boat, was drifting into a gentle breeze.

She sat down by the breakfast table. The radio had turned itself back on again, as it sometimes did. She could never fathom out why – maybe from when she dropped it, perhaps.

And this strange feeling, she realised, was one of relief. As she sank into the chair, it seemed confirmed.

Henry was off somewhere and she was sitting by the Corn Flakes. Tilting the packet, she poured out a larger than usual helping and got up for the milk. She felt oddly hungry.

As she chomped her way through the crunchy flakes, deafened only by her enthusiastic munching, she felt a sudden need.

Having taken in extra breaths during her morning snack, there was a need to expel surplus wind.

Once, when she had suddenly eructated at the breakfast table, she had been severely told off by Henry.

"Unbecoming, unladylike," were the words he used, amongst others. She never belched again, not as far as she knew, having to release the air slowly and surreptitiously in a way that often caused discomfort.

But now, as she realised, Henry was no longer there to reprimand her.

'Wherever ye be, let the wind blow free.'

It could have been one of Archie's sayings and she seemed to hear this piece of advice in a Scottish accent. And once more, she thought of butterfingers.

Glancing at the clock, she heard the belch break forth. It was all the words Henry said it was, as its raucous sound interrupted the unwelcome stillness of the breakfast room. As she gazed around, she seemed to see it reverberate off objects. The noise had sounded so much bigger than she was. And, for a second, it was the sweet serenade of liberty...

Ignoring her statutory obligation to clean her teeth, Elspeth put on her coat and reached for the keys inside her pocket.

The front door closed more softly than usual. She would go and say goodbye, of course. She would say nothing about the burp, although perhaps Henry had heard it – from wherever he was.

Dominic O'Sullivan

The Outside Element

"It's borderline," said Miss Tomkins to Melanie, who was halfway through a cream doughnut.

"What is?"

"Ah, Mark." Miss Tomkins managed to combine surprise with a feeling of guilt. "We were just talking about the department and er... the governors' decision, albeit a narrow one, to carry on with the current A Level syllabus for French."

"Formidable," replied Mark in a French accent. It was strange how words altered their meaning when they went into English.

"However, I *have* to say that the future for literature within the exam framework is far from secure. The governors feel that the Exam Board's enlightened approach towards topics and projects is the way forward."

"Ah yes," said Mark, noticing a blob of jam on Melanie's nose. "Whenever I hear the word 'literature' I reach for my revolver."

"I suppose that's that William Burroughs you're always quoting to us."

"If you say so."

"Anyway, I have to say that the decline in enrolments for certain subjects is a much more pressing case."

"I thought that was why you introduced the 'outside element.'"

He stifled a slight smirk. The 'outside element' was a select group of highly mature students who invariably snoozed through the language classes, only to be stirred occasionally by the odd spontaneous debate.

"We have a duty and commitment to *all* within the community."

"Yes, yes, of course," replied Mark. "It's reassuring to know that money's not a salient issue."

"I've said all I've got to say on the matter," Miss Tomkins replied.

"And put very beautifully," he added.

The following week saw the start of the first class of the autumn term – the new enrolments joined at the hip with the more perennial 'outside' elements.

"Il faut parler tout le temps en français," Mark began.

"Oh yes, I say. Jolly good," said Mr. Crumpshall.

"Et *repondre* en français!"

"Mais oui. Certainly. Bien sure."

Mark sighed. The attempt to conduct entire proceedings in the original language – L1 as Miss. Tomkins was prone to say – never went much beyond the first lesson. The replies of the 'outside element' could not quite adapt and convert comprehension skills into authentic L1 replies. He was floundering on a ship heading for a sandbank of soft options.

"Et vous. Comment vous appelez-vous?"

He addressed one of the younger members of the group, a scruffy, lanky boy whose saving grace was that he was bereft of chewing gum.

Impedes pronunciation, especially in French, Mark would invariably say. And introduces a level of informality which is highly inappropriate.

"Je m'appelle William," said the boy.

"Ah. Guillaume."

"No, William," came the student's reply.

Mark gazed at him. They were an ignorant lot generally, but you should always travel in hope, he thought. And if he had been less concerned with Guillaume's Anglicisation, Mark would have noticed that a second male in the group was quite a rarity as possible companion for Henry Crumpshall.

"Très bien," said Mark.

"Thank you," said Guillaume.

"And now to verb of the week."

"I'm sorry," interrupted Mrs. Rixon-Hicks," but I thought you said we were going to do it all in French."

"Quite right, Patricia," said Mark. "We were, but I wanted to clear up any ambiguity."

"What's ambiguity?" asked Lorraine, who was forty years Patricia's junior. "It sounds a bit dirty."

"Not now," said Mark."We're concentrating on French."

"But I thought it *was* French," queried Lorraine. "Ambiguity. Sounds French, doesn't it?"

"Looks French," said William, who had found it in his dictionary.

"It's the kind of French called Latin."

"Don't be silly," said Lorraine. "How can French be Latin? That's why it's called French, isn't it?"

"I think what he means," interjected Henry Crumpshall, "is that French *derives* from Latin whereas English is…"

"Thank you, Mr.Crumpshall," said Mark.

He looked at the clock. It was almost time for a nap as Mr. Crumpshall invariably fell asleep around three o'clock. He noticed Henry's eyelids starting to droop a fraction, become heavier – an imminently glazed expression beckoning.

"Le verbe du jour," Mark continued.

I thought you said it was 'verb of the week'," said Patricia.

"I did."

"Well, make your mind up!" said Lorraine.

"That's no way to speak!" protested Mrs. Rixon-Hicks.

"It *is* a little confusing," moderated Mr. Crumpshall, who had suddenly woken up again.

"Verbe de la semaine..."

"How did it go?" Miss Tomkins asked Mark at break.
"Not too bad," he replied. "I started off in L1, of course."
"Whose L1," asked Emily Tomkins. "Yours or theirs?"
"Neither," said Mark.
"Any retainers?"
"We've got Henry and Patricia."
"Ah yes. Where would we be without them?"
Down the Job Centre, possibly, he thought.
"There was some lively discussion."
"This is what happens," said Emily, smugly, "When we reach out to all elements of the community!"

"I thought, Mauriac," said Mark later in the week. "For the set text. Nest of Vipers."
"And a play, perhaps?"
"Stella says she doesn't like Molière. She called it Brian Rix in French."
"What about Anouilh? L'alouette?"
"Possibly, though Stella keeps calling him 'ennui'."
"She sounds a little disruptive, that madam!"
"Quite the reverse. She makes things go with a swing. She's streets ahead of everyone else. I shall be sorry to lose her."
"And why would that be?" asked Miss Tomkins looking alarmed. She had a latent phobia of dwindling numbers.
"She's due in three weeks."
Miss Tomkins paused for breath. "Well, she's a naughty girl to get herself in such a mess."
"On the contrary, Emily. She seems quite happy. Oh, and I thought a bit of Voltaire, too."
Emily gave him one of her unhelpful smiles, which she often did when she was about to leave the room with matters unresolved.

She paused for a moment as if gathering her thoughts. "Very well. Mauriac it is, then. Yes, that should be fine."

"All the better with your endorsement."

It was four weeks later when they came to look at Mauriac. A pity, thought Mark, as Stella's comments and perceptions, had she been there, would have enlivened any discussion.

"I don't understand," queried Patricia Rixon-Hicks. "Why do you say 'noeud'?"

"It's a term of abuse, I believe," said Henry, who was still awake.

"That's nerd!" said Lorraine.

"That's what I said," insisted Mrs. Rixon-Hicks.

"I think," said Mark, "we are within inter-lingual confusion."

"I thought it was very clear," said Henry.

"Mrs. Rixon-Hicks is talking about the French," said Mark.

The named lady quickly fluttered her eyelashes. "Patricia, please," she blushed.

"Patricia is referring to the title," explained Mark.

"Yes, but I still don't understand," continued Patricia. "If the final letters in French are silent, why 'noeud'? Shouldn't it be 'ner'?"

"I don't think you can have final letters," said Henry. "It must be in the singular, surely?"

"I was meaning in general," snapped Patricia. "Comme il est pédant!"

Henry tried to get up but sat down again immediately. His right knee appeared to have locked suddenly.

"And I won't take insults directed by an idle housewife who would be better off..."

There was a staggered silence.

"...mounting horses!"

Guillaume giggled.

"Well, really!" said Mrs. Rixon-Hicks. "One expects rudeness from the young but *not...*"

Mark felt intervention was required.

"I don't think Patricia said what you thought she said."

"I distinctly heard. She called me a poof! And I don't even keep cats."

"No, no. Not 'p.d'." He pronounced it 'pay day'. She said pédant."

"Well, that's not much better either," said Henry. "And I refuse to be abused in class by some bored housewife."

"I'm not a housewife," said Patricia. "I have *other* interests."

"Personally, I've never much been interested in Tupperware, if that's what you mean."

"What's Tupperware?" asked Lorraine.

"Ladies and gentlemen!" cried Mark, calling them to order.

"Gentlemen? You're not lumping *me* in with this?" protested William.

"No, no," said Mark, more than ever regretting the enforced departure of Stella. "To go back to the original question..."

"The nerd," said William.

"Precisely. It is 'noeud' because of elision. You remember we talked about this last week. After the 'noeud' there's a 'de', so if you run the two together, you get a 'dee'."

"A 'der', surely?" corrected Henry.

"Does that answer your question, Patricia?"

"Perfectly," she replied, morosely chastened.

"Now I think in the interests of example and as a paradigm of civil behaviour, I think you and Henry should settle your differences and shake hands."

"Very well," said Patricia, who had suddenly noticed that Mark's trousers were quite tight around the rump.

Her latent resistance was weakening. She proffered a reluctant paw in the direction of Henry Crumpshall but her opponent had unexpectedly fallen asleep.

"How was it?" Emily asked later that day.
"We didn't exactly get very far," said Mark.
"The Mauriac?"
"Yes."
"I thought so. Projects are so much easier to teach. There's little room for opinions and interpretation."
"At least we've got the title sorted," said Mark.
"The title?"
"Mrs. Rixon-Hicks got into a muddle with the title and had an argument with Henry."
"What about?"
"The title."
"The title? Henry?"
"Mr. Crumpshall."
"Ah yes. So he's still here, then?"
"Yes. Most of the time. Anyway, he misheard a comment of Patricia's and took offence. I had to intervene."
"No damage, then?"
"Well, Patricia was a little testy."
"We have to remember, of course, that Edwin is both governor and benefactor of the college."
"Edwin. What's that got to do with it?"
"Edwin Rixon-Hicks. Patricia's husband."
"Oh I see. So we mustn't do anything to rock the boat or offend Patricia?"
"We are continually indebted to them for their support. And after all, Henry's been going to language classes for years!"
"Well, so has Patricia. She keeps alternating between French and Spanish, both *my* subjects incidentally, and frequently mixing the two."

"Even so, we must be mindful of the situation," said Emily.

"That all students are equal but some are..."

"Precisely," replied Emily.

For the following few weeks Mauriac, Voltaire and the Drainage System in Northern France, the selected topic, alternated in class.

"I was always interested in drains," said Henry. "Ever since I was a child. We had a holiday in Great Yarmouth."

"No doubt you can recall some of your experiences," said Mark, encouragingly.

"I'm afraid not," said Henry. "I can't remember a thing. But it was a lovely holiday."

"Well, thank you, Henry," Mark replied. "Now today I thought we would look at the tradition of anti-clericalism in France as a relevant background to our book."

"Wasn't Voltaire a Catholic?" enquired Patricia.

"Yes, but today's Friday," said Henry.

"I don't see the relevance," she replied a touch icily.

"Friday's the day we do the other fella," said Henry.

"Oh," said Patricia. "I was *particularly* looking forward to Voltaire."

"What does Voltaire mean?" Lorraine asked.

"It means Friday," said William.

Patricia was confused. "Does it? Well then, it would be quite apt to do *him*, then."

"We did Voltaire on Wednesday," said William.

"Ah yes," said Patricia. "That was when I had my riding lesson."

"I've got a quote," said Henry, mercifully ignoring Patricia's last remark. "It happens to be a Voltaire one."

"Well, perhaps we could hear that," Mark suggested, hoping that dust would settle on the 'riding lesson'. "And then we'll move on to François..."

"He means Mauriac," said William, sensing Lorraine's confusion.

"Thank you," said Mark, who noticed that William seemed more alert than usual.

"Pas croyant, pas practiquant, mais catholique!" announced Henry and successfully sat down again.

"Thank you, Henry," said Mark.

"Je vous en prie," Henry beamed.

"Couldn't we do half Voltaire and half Mauriac?" Patricia suggested. "There may be some interesting parallels."

"We haven't really time, I'm afraid," said Mark. "We must crack on with our Vipers."

For the next two weeks, Voltaire and the drainage project were largely sidelined.

"Progress?" asked Emily.

"We're getting there," said Mark. "I must say, it does make a difference having an additional male in the class."

"You mean William O'Driscoll?"

"Yes. Wod."

"Pardon?"

"His friends call him 'Wod'."

"I think you're having me on!"

"So you don't believe in it, then?"

Miss Tomkins failed to give a reply so Mark continued on about the additional dynamics of not having an exclusively female audience.

"If the class isn't too early in the morning, then William *does* make some pertinent comments. Though, of course, it doesn't make up for the loss of Stella."

Miss Tomkins shuddered. "Your appreciation is misplaced. I used to find that girl very unforthcoming."

"The brighter ones are always difficult."

"As I say, I found no evidence of that."

It was Friday afternoon and Henry, who had been looking out of the window, was nodding off.

"The writer expresses deep distaste for his pious family in this chapter," Mark revealed.

"Don't spoil the surprise for us," said William.

"I would have thought the early chapters already established the prevailing mood," Mark replied.

"If you say so," said William, sulkily.

"I think it's always good to have the author's thoughts explained to us," said Mrs. Rixon-Hicks, rushing to Mark's rescue. "Especially when one is groping with another language."

"What do you mean, groping?" asked Henry, who had unexpectedly reawakened.

"Precisely that," said Mrs. Rixon-Hicks, who had not entirely forgotten her last spat with Mr. Crumpshall. "Coming to terms with the writer's layers of meaning," she continued, "we so often seek enlightenment."

Henry cast his eyes upwards. "I feel a sermon coming on."

"Well..." said Mark, trying to keep the peace between the two factions and noticing that William had taken over Henry's job of looking out of the window.

He looked at the names on the dwindling register and for the first time noticed that William had Seamus as a second first name. Coming from a devout Irish background, he supposed that William might be able to shed some light on the subject.

"William," said Mark, endeavouring to distract the boy's thoughtful contemplation of a pair of herring gulls, "I'm assuming that you had a good Catholic background. Anything you particularly remember from your religious education?"

Whether it was Patricia's word 'groping' that did it, Mark was not entirely sure. For a moment, William looked blank, as he invariably did, and then suddenly sprang into life.

"There was one thing..."

"You can share it with us," beamed Mark.

"Well, when my brother was at school, they used to skip the Sixth Commandment in Religious Studies."

Mark and Henry both embarked on a swift deduction exercise.

"I should *think* not!" exclaimed Mrs. Rixon-Hicks.

William gave her a pained look and continued.

"When my brother Donal was there it wasn't taught or anything. Just glossed over."

"I'm not surprised," said Mr. Crumpshall. "Typical repressive censorship!"

"Well, anyway, we had this so-called 'enlightened' priest, though he was a funny kind of bloke. Never washed his cassock. Smelled like a compost heap."

"Do go on," encouraged Mark. He was glad that William's sulk was now over.

"Anyway, one morning, second period, he comes up with this bit of advice... Out of nowhere, it was. 'When you're in the bath', he said, 'and getting aroused, just cry out, sweet angels help me!'"

There was a prolonged Thursday afternoon silence.

"Sounds rather naughty to me," said Mr. Crumpshall. "Bit blasphemous!"

"I was *asked* to remember," insisted William.

"No, no. Not *you*, laddie. This priest fellow. It sounds most extraordinary!"

Mark turned towards the strangely silent Mrs. Rixon-Hicks, who was as immobile as a pillar. A vivid scarlet blush had spread to the roots of her chestnut-tinted hair.

"Er...thank you for that...William," said Mark, nervously. "Erm, I think we should press on."

"It doesn't stand up to close scrutiny," remarked Mr. Crumpshall.

Mark saw Patricia visibly wince.

"I'm afraid French is off this autumn," said Emily two months later, in her demure yet venomous way.

"The literature class?"

"Yes. I regret to say we've lost one of our stalwarts. She's written to say that she's joined the raffia and basket-weaving group instead. It's 'less controversial.' *Her* words."

But Mark was barely listening, for through the staffroom window, he witnessed a welcome sight. A woman was pushing a pram across the grass, slowly towards the main entrance.

"Stella!" he said.

Dominic O'Sullivan

Pennies

He wondered whether he would come. Whether today meant that he really would. His fingers alighted on the door handle, which yielded slowly, unwillingly. The room was in half-light; the best time maybe for such things.. To the left, the curtains partly drawn gave the sense of being in attendance, of waiting. As usual, Edward cast his eyes around. Nothing had changed or been moved.

Being the first day of the holidays, Justin had wanted to go down to the sea front. It was into a chilly wind in April as they descended the slope that led away from the pavilion. Pausing halfway down, the assembled roofs of kiosks and stalls made it seem like some miniature, slumbering city. As if awaiting some kiss or breath of life, a burst of renewal.

As it was, the droplets of rain from the early showers only gave it a more dejected appearance. Some of the signs indicating the proud owners of various stalls or the function of certain rides had slipped onto one side, unhinged by the gusty, nagging wind. Unhinged.

The hand that tugged in his pocket propelled him ever further down the slope, dragging him on with a sense of urgency.

He sat on a chair by the window looking out onto the windswept garden. Some trees were always the first to go he noticed, while others with their few remaining leaves hung obstinately on. The wind blew them in squally flurries, so as mini tornadoes the leaves whirled around the edge of the house beyond the shed.

One summer, he had moved some of his office things there, thinking that he would be disturbed less, that he could get on with and concentrate on his work. It made little difference. Justin could always sense when he was not inside the house, even without knocking on the study door. Instead, he would come running out into the garden, often in the pouring rain, with a question that needed answering there and then or with something that he wanted to show him.

"You look like a drowned mouse," Edward said to him.

Justin gazed up at him and smiled. "Have you ever seen a drowned mouse?" he asked.

"Not really."

"So how can you say I look like a drowned mouse, then?"

"Because of your hair. It's all brown and spiky."

He lifted him up for a moment, drips and all, in the musty, makeshift office.

Together they ran back towards the house, torrential rain cascading off the path, and up to the comparative warmth of the bathroom where immediately he reached for a towel to rub the boy down.

"You should know better than to go outside when it's raining!"

His plea was ignored. "I wanted to show you this," he said. He held out a trembling, excited arm. Clasped in his tiny hand was a large bronze penny.

"Where did you find it?"

"Upstairs in the loft."

"Oh."

"What is it, dad?" Justin asked solemnly.

He turned the penny over and saw the faint outline. "It's a bun penny," he said.

Justin looked at him in disbelief. "I can't see a bun," he said." So how can it be a bun penny?"

Edward pointed to the vague shape of the face. "Look at the lady's hair. See, it's all tied up into a bun." His finger traced the outline of Victoria's profile.

"Is it very old?" Justin asked.

"Quite old."

"How old?" Justin asked, peering at the barely discernible face.

Edward flipped the coin over to check the date.

"What's her name?" Justin asked without waiting for a reply to his other question.

"Victoria," he said.

"And is she a queen?" Justin asked.

"The longest serving queen we had," Edward replied.

"Do queens last a long time?"

Edward nodded. "This one did. Shall we take a look up in the loft? See if we can find any more?" The small hand in his dragged him eagerly upstairs.

They searched through the slumbering treasures of the attic but no more coins revealed themselves.

It was not long afterwards that he decided to plant old coins throughout the house – pre-decimal relics to test the boy's powers of deduction. Whenever Justin discovered the various pennies and shillings, he wanted to know all about the faces he could see. He began to unravel the relationships between the monarchs, to remember their dates. Many a dessert or after dinner coffee was punctuated with squeals of delight from upstairs as another penny was being discovered.

Each time now, when he found a coin buried in the settee or camouflaged against the intricate patterns of the carpet, he thought of him. Pennies from heaven. Lying in wait...Waiting.

He glanced back from the garden, from the view of the shed whose roof was in need of repair, and the steady afternoon drizzle. He felt the need to pace up and down the room; the room that had once served as an office before the planned evacuation to the shed.

It had only been for a moment that April day; a split second. As they walked along the promenade, he had stopped to look out to sea. In the distance, smoke was unfurling from a boat on the horizon, a dark, inky smudge on a canopy of blue. And if he'd brought the glasses with them, they could have peered out at the wheeling birds beyond the breakwaters, watched the black and white plumage of the strutting oystercatchers.

Justin had run on beyond the last of the boarded-up ice cream kiosks and towards the line of beach huts. He liked to hide amongst them or behind them, venturing out suddenly to surprise him.

He was trying to work out which one he was most likely to hide behind when it saw it out of the corner of his eye, careering towards the shore. In seconds, the huts were buried under a violent plume of spray that hit the promenade and then steepled upwards. For a moment, he stood still, immobile in disbelief. It couldn't have happened; couldn't have been like that.

As the wave receded, he could see that some of the beach huts were lying now on their sides, toppled into submission by the sudden, unforgiving force.

He rushed towards the remaining huts, playing now in the frantic game of hide and seek. Perhaps it was the red and white one, or the larger sky-blue...

The waves still battered the shore but nothing equalled the sudden unexpected volley that had brought down and decapitated half the beach huts.

He circled them, searching them for hours, walking back and forth, calling him, crying out...

It was half past three, he noticed. The time Justin would always be at home. Just back from school. His hurried footsteps taking delight in the welcome sense of freedom, talking to whoever was there for him.

The fading light gave way to the gradual onset of darkness.

And for a moment, he wondered if Justin would come — come running into the room. There was always a chance. Maybe.

Silent Plunder

"It's given us a great deal of trouble," remarked Henry during the monthly meeting.

"I always said it should have been controlled at the time. When it was first spotted," replied Miss Meldreth. "And now it's quite rampant. A bit like men," she added.

Henry glanced across at Gillian Meldreth with his studied pained expression. There was no reciprocal word for misogyny, he thought, though perhaps it was now overdue. Just like the action regarding the dreaded weed that had been terrorising the county.

Miss Meldreth sat back in her chair, slightly more relaxed. She was usually more comfortable, sat more languidly after her 'swipe'. Her features took on a calm, vacant, some would say glazed expression, which Henry found oddly attractive.

"Which is why we have brought in Professor Takaki Hakimoto," he announced.

Professor Hakimoto sat opposite Miss Meldreth, comprehending little. On hearing his name he bowed slightly and smiled.

Miss Meldreth glanced up at the bulky portrait above Henry's head. The frame looked dangerously heavy and would deliver a hefty wallop if it tumbled from its place on the wall. There was always hope, she thought.

Henry, oblivious to Councillor Meldreth's psychopathic intentions, continued his carefully rehearsed speech. He paused midway to give the illusion that it sounded natural, yet anyone peeping through the chink in his curtains the previous

Dominic O'Sullivan

evening, would have seen a declamatory hand and an unfettered tummy proclaiming loudly to a long wall mirror and armchair nestling next to a piano.

"To combat this nuisance, this horticultural scourge dumped on us by those thoughtless and inconsiderate Victorian botanists from the previous century…"

At this point, Councillor Brimstow felt obliged to interrupt. "As it is the first decade of the twenty-first, sir, that statement is woefully incorrect."

"You know what I mean," retorted Henry, annoyed that his carefully selected range of adjectives had been sabotaged.

"And as Honorary President of the Wibbleswick Museum, I feel somewhat incensed that so much blame should be laid at the doorstep of the pioneering Victorians."

Walter Brimstow looked in Professor Hakimoto's direction and stared appealingly at him for approval.

"It's nothing more than a garden escape," intervened Gillian. "A careless male oversight."

"I think we should return," said Henry, with a small dramatic pause, "to the problem in question."

Professor Hakimoto gazed inscrutably at the unwieldy portrait on the wall. People here were too large, he thought. The inflated alderman seemed to have an unconfined spread, which in turn appeared to have been taken up by most of the committee. Even the lady member was a bit on the podgy side.

"Knotweed," said Henry.

"Which weed?" queried Walter.

"I've just said it," replied Henry.

"Did you? I'm afraid I didn't catch it."

"I think Councillor Brimstow heard 'what weed?'" suggested Coralie O'Reilly helpfully. It was her task to take the minutes of the meetings whilst offering tactful, hinting glances at the clock.

"I feel it is inappropriate to waste time," said Henry, pompously. "Professor Hakimoto has come to us at great expense. If you had scrutinised the agenda, Walter, you would have seen that it clearly states Knotweed, Japanese."

Walter stared meekly back.

"And now we must move on. We have before us a very exciting development which Professor Hakimoto has put before us."

"Well?" said Gillian, coldly.

"To combat the invasive threat which tears up concrete, invades paths and railway embankments and causes so much destructive damage..."

Walter, who had a keen ear for tautology, wondered whether he should query the last two words but thought better of it. There was no doubt some apologia somewhere for constructive damage and his mind wandered off to the Pendlebury Shopping Mall, which was possibly one of the Council's greatest blunders, and for which his uncle, as an obdurate Independent, had been partly responsible.

"We have the *bug*!" announced Henry, grandly.

"I'm so sorry," attempted Miss Meldreth sympathetically.

"A bug which, as Professor Hakimoto assures us, will deal sufficient damage and control to the alien invader."

"And where is the bug from?" asked Miss Meldreth.

"Hakitaiko Sudachiki," Professor Hakimoto replied eagerly.

There was no answer to this snippet of information other than a soft 'Ooh!' of approbation, and the professor sat back in his chair with a sense of achievement and accomplishment.

"You're willing to risk this?" continued Gillian.

"We've tried everything else!" said Henry. "We must! The weed is pushing up buildings, undermining roads..."

"Yes," said Gillian. "As you mentioned previously. And when do we get to meet the bug?"

Henry looked over to Professor Hakimoto. "I think we can safely say Wednesday of next week."

Professor Hakimoto smiled graciously and the meeting consequently broke up.

"I was very glad of your assistance," Henry said afterwards to Professor Hakimoto in the Dog and Duck.

He nodded peremptorily, more interested in examining the contents of his beer glass.

"Is everything okay?" Henry asked him.

"I think something in my beer. Something froating."

Henry looked at the pale liquid from which Professor Hakimoto had taken a delicate sip.

"It's the yeast, I expect. I'll get Peggy to change it."

"No, no," his colleague insisted. "I do not want to cause scandal."

"It's no problem. I'm sure Peggy'll change it."

Hakimoto glanced across to the busy bar.

"This woman better."

"Better?"

"Yes."

"Better? Better than what?"

"Better than your colleague lady in Chamber."

"You mean Gillian?"

"Yes. I think so."

The noise in the Dog and Duck suddenly reached a shrill crescendo.

"Her blests are froppy."

Henry choked momentarily on his beer.

"Pardon?"

"Her blests are froppy," the professor repeated.

As once having taught English for a week somewhere near Bognor Regis, Henry was familiar with the Japanese inability to distinguish between 'l' and 'r'.

"I wouldn't have thought you would have noticed..."

"Notice? Yes, of course. When too much talking going on and noise, which I cannot always understand, I look around for female comfort and..."

Henry looked in alarm at the impassive Hakimoto.

"It was *big* disappointment for me."

"Well," said Henry. "We'll see if the electorate can maybe sharpen up on their choice of candidates."

"You have erection coming?" the professor asked.

Henry gazed deeply into Hakimoto's pint.

"I think I *will* go and change it for you," he said.

After an unexpected delay, the professor returned three weeks later with a retinue of scientists carrying a large white box under each arm.

"It is the answer to your pright," he announced solemnly to Henry.

"I hope so." He gazed at the impassive bearers of pale boxes.

"And how many bugs per box?"

"About two hundred," said the professor.

"And will that be enough?" Henry asked.

"More than enough. This insect likes sex too much. Two hundred is soon five hundred. And five hundred is... Well, weed will be all gone."

"I hope so," Henry replied. "Of course, we're very excited about it."

"About sex or insect?" enquired the professor.

"Well, insect, of course," said Henry.

"Ah yes. I lecall meeting. There was no clumpet if I lemember."

"Well, yes. Maybe not."

The scientists all walked to the individual cars that were waiting for them to take them from the airport.

"If accident happen, then all will be lost," the professor announced calmly. "But if many cars, plobabirity not so big."

"Indeed."

"And where are we going?" Professor Hakimoto asked.

"To Claypitts Green."

The professor nodded. "Good choosing?"

"Yes. It has been selected as the historic area, the release site for these welcome carnivores of knotweed. I believe there's a large clump behind the cricket pavilion."

"We make history, then?" the professor smiled.

"Yes, indeed," Henry replied. "Of course, Claypitts knows nothing about this. It's all very hush-hush."

And he put a finger to his lips.

In a little over two hours they were alighting from the smooth limousines.

"Very nice," the professor exclaimed as he stepped out of the car. The village green with the cordoned-off cricket pitch awaited their attention.

"Behind shed, you say?"

"Yes."

"Top secret!" The professor laughed. "It feel as if we do something naughty."

"On the contrary," his host said. "We are doing something of great benefit to..."

The white boxes were opened at exactly the same time and placed under the heavy stalks of the weed. A few quick taps and a number of disgruntled insects emerged to dine on the thick stems that towered above them. There were a few petulant buzzes and then all was quiet.

Some three weeks later, a distraught call came from Mrs. Olive Parsley to the Claypitts Green Horticultural Society.

"It's my dahlias," she stormed. "They've been eaten almost to the ground! It's clearly sabotage from my rivals!"

But within an hour, Olive's rivals were also ringing up with the same story. In fact, for many miles across the county not a dahlia was left to be seen. It made front news on the Wibbleswick Gazette.

And so it was, when the village cricketers had finally trudged over to the Spade and Buckett, that Henry shone his torch behind the cricket pavilion. He gazed slowly upwards. The clump of knotweed had barely been touched and, in fact, many new shoots had sprung up from behind the groundsman's hut.

The following spring, a number of brightly coloured catalogues were delivered to the Claypitts Green area and a string of other villages.

Mrs. Parsley picked up her copy with interest. 'The star bargain', the brochure proudly proclaimed, 'is the new Knotweed Bug-free Dahlia with its inbuilt immunity to the silent assassin. If ordered now, it could arrive just in time to plant for the various lovely autumn flower shows. Hurry! Demand expected to be very huge!'

The form just below bore the supplier's name. 'Happy hunting,' it said 'from home of Japanese flower garden. Hakitaiko Sudachiki.'

Dominic O'Sullivan

The Moment

Ute's chair was slightly nearer than usual – about three inches. Daniel cast a glance behind him to see if his seat had been pushed away from the wall, but no, everything seemed the same.

"Is it bothering you?" she asked him.

He shook his head.

She could see that it was. "It's the desk," she said. "The cleaners must have moved it round."

"Maybe," he said.

It seemed strange to think of cleaners going about their business, changing things, mopping the floor in *their* room. The room where they attempted to...

She stood up and pushed the desk further back with her legs and bottom. Now it looked as if she was too far away. Ute circumspectly slid the chair back towards Daniel. The expression on his face showed it was better.

"You must be pleased," she said when they had nearly finished. "Going home."

"Yes," he said.

He was gazing beyond her, past the silent streaks of rain that were starting to wriggle their way down the rectangular window panes. They hadn't yet obscured the view of the park with its trees turning colour. Autumn, he thought. It had been a good time of year until...

"What were you thinking about?" she suddenly asked him.

"Nothing much," he said.

"Remember what we said last time," Ute said. "That's what we agreed on. That was to be the plan."

Uncomfortably, he shifted his gaze from the glass, away from the teasing lure of memory, letting Ute's pale, studious face and shock of brown hair obscure the dwindling light beyond.

It was a pity she couldn't go back with him, he thought, as some benevolent kind of shadow. A therapeutic angel. Someone on hand to talk to, discuss things, protect him from the complications of this new way of life.

Perhaps he was in the present now; with Ute's help, her physical shape was blotting out, locking away any associations.

"It's difficult," he replied.

"I know."

"There seem to be a thousand memories, as if I approach the house each time from a new angle – like umpteen takes in a film."

She gazed at him for a moment. "What will you do?" she said.

"My cousin," said Daniel. "He's offered me a place to stay. For a few weeks anyway. Gather my thoughts. Readjust."

She smiled.

"But I thought you just said 'Live in the present'."

It was a mild rebuke to her.

"You know what I meant. Of course there must be *some* future. Plans, arrangements. Obviously for when you leave here."

There! She'd said the word again. Only 'leave' sounded more urgent than 'going home', which, in any case, was inappropriate. It couldn't be done. Was no longer there. No longer existed. 'Leave' sounded like being ejected from a club. A termination of some kind of agreement.

"Yes," Daniel said.

"It's the past that needs separating, leaving behind. Not dwelling on what's *been*. Going forward. And being easier on yourself, too."

"Forgiveness, you mean?" he said.

"If you like. We all need to forgive. It's part of the healing process."

"Forgive and forget," sighed Daniel, shifting between the wooden arms of the chair.

Sometimes he would place both hands forward on the ends of the chair and lift himself slightly upwards, arching his back, contorting himself like a cat. He no longer indulged in this, but in the beginning, when he had spent those early days in conversation with Ute, he did, sniffing round her in a way as if to gain her measure – to figure her out. She would sit and wait for him to settle down again, her soft, enquiring voice held in reserve to question and then reassure him.

Only once did she become impatient. "You'll get back ache," she remarked as he slumped back into the chair. They moved on.

The rain obscured everything now beyond the window; the parkland drenched in a soft veil of grey.

"Can I come back to see you?" he asked her.

She reached inside the desk for a moment. She was holding out a white piece of paper to him.

"What's this?" he asked her.

"It's my colleague, Mary McGlachlan. She'll be available if you need to..."

"But not *you*?"

"I have my work *here*. Besides, it would mean you coming back and it sounds like quite a trek from where you'll be staying."

"I didn't tell you where he lived."

"You know how inaccessible this place is."

"I believe so."

The old asylum philosophy. He looked away.

"You're angry."

"I'm being cut off. It seems too soon."

"No one's casting you off, Daniel. Believe me. But to come back *here*, to come back *here* would be..."

"Retrograde?"

"Very likely!"

"Not living in the present?"

"I'm sorry, Daniel. It's all arranged."

She had her pleading look on. He could see her line of reasoning, quite clearly in fact, though it still came as a bit of a shock. The links severed.

He looked back at her. He had no wish to spend their last time together with bad feelings...in an argument or dissent...

"Mary McGlachlan sounds like a malt whisky," he said.

Ute smiled. "Give her a chance. If you need her at any time."

"I might not. You know, move on and all that. Live in the present."

She glanced up at the clock. It was nearly time. She moved towards him.

"I wish you all the best, Daniel. I really do."

He leaned forward and kissed her. The first time he had kissed a woman in eight years.

"Thanks, Ute."

"You're welcome, Daniel."

The door closed. He had left her behind a desk – well, not actually at the time, but some minutes later when she would change chairs to attend to the pile of paperwork. She was trapped in that room; tied to all the demands of her patients or 'clients' as most of them preferred to call them. It made her sound like a tart. Patient was a better word – from the French 'patienter'. And Daniel had been one of those who'd duly waited and now his turn had come. Tomorrow, he would walk out of here, just as he was walking away from her now, along and under the subdued lighting of the corridor while Ute was still chained to the demands and burdens of her desk.

The next morning, he got up early, feeling an excess of butterflies in his stomach. He ate his breakfast, made the rest of his goodbyes to Joe and Chris, Lenny and Sue, and let the taxi that had come for him glide past the clinic gates, without turning round to look back once. Ute would have been proud, he thought, seeing as he was following her suggestion.

But it was hard and in the wing mirror he caught a grudging glimpse of the building receding, as if looking down the wrong end of the telescope. A bend in the road and it was gone. Had vanished.

He picked up the keys to his cousin's house from a shop in the village.

"I'll walk from here," he said to the taxi driver.

"You know the way?" the man asked expectantly.

He hadn't got any coins ready to give him a tip, and besides, it seemed to be too early to be doing such things. Different things.

Daniel drew some money from the cash machine, aware of being watched by the next in line. He stuffed the notes into his jacket pocket and carried on up the hill with his light suitcase. He would need more clothes, he thought. But that would do another day. Take the train into one of the bigger towns, indulge in the ultimate therapy.

Cash had accumulated nicely in the bank during his absence; interest rates weren't too bad. He could stock himself up with a whole new wardrobe if he wanted.

He turned the next corner and there he was. The bay-windowed semi was set back from the road. A mossy, winding path partly covered by a large rhododendron bush. It hinted of high rainfall, as did the ferns nestling by the sides of the house; more rainfall even than where he had been gazing out onto daily views of lush parkland.

Daniel placed the key in the lock. It turned very stiffly as if unused to such an intrusion. For a moment, he endured a panic thinking it was the wrong key. The third effort saw the door yield and he stepped inside. There was a smell of expectancy as well as that of emptiness; of absent ownership, of waiting, willing someone to arrive. It also smelt slightly damp and musty so he went upstairs to open the windows.

Lionel had suggested he use the end room. It had the best view he said. Neighbouring houses were concealed beneath whispering poplars and the edge of the hill. Only the odd plume of smoke hinted at habitation and the presence of someone else. The nearby hills were covered in bracken and they too were turning rusty brown in the late October sun.

It was quiet. He listened to the stillness of the house. Even the road was silent. Nothing. Not a sound whereas the clinic had been full of noises, of doors banging, endless footsteps and voices in the corridors, the rattling of plates in the communal dining room.

And now he was free of all that, of the lack of privacy, of enforced company, of meetings. And of Ute. He wondered what she would be doing now. Sitting with her replacement patient, unravelling the complexities of his troubled brow; sitting in the same chair and he gazing out beyond her and onto the waving, beckoning trees of the park.

Once he had seen a deer gazing outside his window. It was early morning and there were layers of mist that crept and unfurled their way towards the meadows. He had moved closer to the window and the animal, sensing sudden movement, had turned and fled. At times he asked himself whether he had dreamt it; early morning, mist, sleeping, waking.

Daniel wondered if there would be wildlife here, too. Maybe not deer but foxes; an owl to sing outside his window. Later, when he walked round the garden, he noticed how damp the soil was. The uncut grass was thick and lush. At the bottom he could hear the faint rustling of a stream. The shed underneath the willow tree was not locked and was well stocked with implements. He could tidy up the garden for Lionel, sweep away the leaves, manicure the wilting roses.

It was when he went to put back the hoe which he had knocked off the wall that he saw it – the two containers.

The evening was late when he had crept back towards the house. The curtains in the upstairs room were drawn; everything in darkness. He moved silently across the lawn, carrying something in his right hand. Undoing the stopper, he poured the contents through the cat flap. The cat was no doubt out on its nocturnal run, indulging in its ritual, addictive night of slaughter of smaller, helpless animals. He wondered whether for a moment it might be inside, exulting in its general routine of idleness. Sleeping, hunting, sleeping. Hopefully, it wasn't. He had nothing against the cat; little argument with her – no case of suspected infidelity.

And then he saw Julie with Mark, fixed in his mind's eye, laughing, disrobing, laughing at him from a distance. It was then that he dropped the match.

The house was barely habitable after that. Julie had stayed out that evening, not getting home till two in the morning, returning to the shock of the fire brigade, the flickering remains.

One week later, he walked into Burnside Police Station and told them all. He hadn't known what came over him – what had happened, what he meant to do. Yes, thank heaven, Julie wasn't in the house!

Arson, it clearly was. A period of absence. An attempt to unravel it all. And finally, the Clinic, which got down to the nitty-gritty, and Ute.

He turned away from the red containers of paraffin, no doubt for the small heaters in the breakfast and laundry room. He wouldn't visit the shed again, not wanting to re-ignite memories. Just go forward. Eat breakfast in cooler temperatures, do the garden as best he could.

The air was invigorating at his cousin's, the house companionable. But clearly he couldn't stay there forever. During the next few weeks, he would get the papers; see what there was in the way of accommodation. Find something through an agency.

It was a while before he got it. Some places inevitably reminded him of Julie. The patterns of brickwork or the way the house was set back from the road. The house. Their house! The house that in the end had betrayed him on more than one occasion and had had to be sacrificed.

Finally, he found a neutral place – nothing that harked back. Be and live in the present. Her advice, of course. Got a job with a firm of architects. Ironic, then, that the designer of houses, should, in the last eight years have been guilty of demolishing one. But no, everything was going well from the work point of view.

One evening he had finished early and decided to take a different way home. The meandering street with its hotchpotch of buildings took him down towards the river, the smarter side of town. By the converted mill, the darker waters of the river reflected a secluded bar with welcome lights glowing. One drink after a hard day's work seemed a reasonable recompense.

Once inside, the interior was plush and spacious unlike the pub they went to sometimes on the corner after work. Music throbbed in the background; candles on the tables gently flickered. There were one or two couples perched in alcoves behind him. They spoke to each other mutedly as if their utterances had drowned in the lavish carpet at their feet.

He was aware of movement; there was someone at his side.

"Do you mind if I join you?"

She was pulling up a stool next to him as he sat at the bar. For a moment he was no longer a single item, becoming a fleeting couple too. Angie was in no hurry, it seemed. She ordered a second drink for herself.

"I really should be going," Daniel said.

She must have noticed his lack of conviction. "Are you meeting someone?" she asked. "Have you got to get back for anything?"

He shook his head.

"So where's the rush?" she said and smiled.

Her long fair hair took on the soft candlelight of the bar.

"This place is bigger than you think," said Daniel looking around.

"Of course," Angie said. "What with all the gaming rooms."

"The gaming rooms?"

"Yes. There's a small casino out the back. Didn't you see the signs?"

He hadn't. It was the first time. The first time he had deviated from his work to home trail.

"Are you going to play, then?" she asked him.

"Play what?" Daniel said.

"Playing whatever's inside."

"And what *is* inside?"

"There's only one way to find out," she smiled again.

Lightly supporting his arm, she guided him towards the doors beyond the bar. Behind the thick drapes that further muffled sound, he saw the spread of gaming tables, the roulette, the stooping croupier, and further away the dice players and card tables.

"It's nice," she said and sat down, patting the chair he was about to descend on.

The croupier threw her a wink.

"I've not really played before," Daniel began. "You know..."

"Of course not," she said. "There's a first time for everything, isn't there? But I can help you. Start you off. People get..."

She didn't finish her sentence, or if she did, he didn't hear it.

There were Ute's words in his ears as he looked away from the containers of paraffin – the two containers he had come across that afternoon in the shed.

"The present," Ute was saying. "That's where you have to be. Aim to be in the present. Forget..."

And in this unexpectedly vast arena of gaming tables, with its roulette wheel, mesmerising him like a giant eye, there was *only* the present; the feelings and sensations of the heightened moment.

He was comfortable where he sat. Angie was at his side. A warm glow surrounded him now.

He would give himself over to the promise...and expectations of the moment.

Switzerland

"What time did you say? Sheila asked him.
"I can't remember if I did," said David.
"You know, for Hedwiga."
"It's Ludmila."
"Ludmila, then."
"Let me see the note again."

David was getting flustered. He hastily scoured the kitchen for an envelope that had a stamp depicting the High Tatras.

"I can't find it."

"It might be caught up in the ironing board," Sheila suggested.

"The ironing board?"

"I was ironing when you showed it to me. You *never* put anything away."

"That's not true!" he protested.

During the altercation Martin came into the kitchen.

"Is anything wrong?" he asked.

"He can't find the letter," said Sheila.

"What letter?"

"Camilla's."

"It's Ludmila!"

"What is?" said Martin.

"The letter."

"A letter called Ludmila. I see."

"The new au-pair. She's arriving today."

"Oh that," said Martin, nonchalantly. "It's by the phone."

"Why didn't you say so?"

"Because for most of the time you were talking nonsense."

"That's no way to talk," snapped Sheila.

Anxiety was temporarily interrupted as they united to rebuke Martin.

"Well, get it, David!" said Sheila.

David reached for the tray on which the telephone sat.

"Hell's teeth!" he exclaimed on looking at the letter. "She's coming at five! Today!"

"What time is it now?"

"Ten to. I'll never make it. It'll take me at least half an hour."

"Good job I came when I did. The poor girl would be rotting in a ditch somewhere till you lot got your act together."

Martin avoided the tea-towel that was lobbed in his direction. David was panicking, searching for the car keys.

"They were last on my desk," he said.

"Why don't I go?" Martin suggested. "It won't take much longer on my bike. I mean, by the time you've stopped pratting around it'll be time for her to go home again."

He left the kitchen before anything else could be hurled at him. Inside the garage, with its smell of leaking oil, the bicycle rested against a wall. From within he could still hear exasperated protests of, "I'm sure I put them down earlier on the table!"

He sighed. Parents were so embarrassing really, especially when they tried to gain kudos by being so unreasonably bossy.

The wind blew in his face, ruffling his hair, as he cycled down the narrow hedgerow lanes.

"He can't bring her back, can he?" said Sheila after Martin had gone. "It's too far to walk."

"He can tell her I'm on my way," said David, pocketing the object of his search.

"You found them, then?" said Sheila.

"Yes, I found them."

"If that bike folds up, they could always get a taxi."

She had a vision of a frantic Ludmila at the lonely railway station, with no staff to come to her rescue. How was her English, anyway? Would she be able to make herself understood?

It was around five twenty when Martin cycled into the station forecourt. A lone, squat figure was sitting patiently on a bench.

"Are you Ludmila?" he asked.

"Yes," she said, surprised. "You know my name!"

"We were expecting you. I'm so sorry about the delay."

"It's okay," said Ludmila. "I go to the toilet. It's quite nice for a station. But you are too young to have the family!"

"No, no," said Martin. "The old man couldn't find his car keys."

"Which old man?" asked Ludmila. "Your grandfather live with you?"

"No, no. The old fella."

"I am not understanding. Some old man didn't come?"

At that moment David's car swung into the deserted station approach. He got out to meet them.

"I'm so sorry, Ludmila," he began. "Engine trouble?"

"No," she replied. The train was very good. Fine, in fact."

"Hop in," said David. "Marty, stick your bike in the back."

"I can cycle, dad. It's okay."

"Do as you're told!"

"Mmm. Your grandfather has nice car," Ludmila said to Martin. "But maybe too big for this road."

Branches scraped against the side windows. At the ford at the bottom of the hill, David took the descent too fast and water cannoned against the bonnet.

"There is a whale in the road," observed Ludmila, meaning 'well'.

"It's a ford, actually," replied David.

"I thought whale was quite appropriate," said Martin. "How many times do you forget it's there?"

"It is no good," said Ludmila, "to have such a thing in the road. I was once in Albania..."

"Here we are," said David as the farmhouse came into view. "You must be hungry."

"No sanks," replied Ludmila. "But I need toilet. I ate pound of plums while waiting for that train. And then at station."

"Fair enough," said Martin. "Let no man stand in your way."

"That'll do, Martin," said David.

"It is most kind, your grandson."

"There, you see," said Martin smugly.

They showed Ludmila up to her room but on spotting the bathroom, she immediately dived in.

"She seems a nice girl," commented Sheila, ignoring the frequencies of Ludmila's bowels.

They had a simple supper of bread and soup.

"It is very good," said Ludmila. She looked at the clock. It was nearly half past eight.

"And now I think I am going to bed," she announced.

"So soon?" queried David. "Stay for a while."

"She's probably tired, dear," said Sheila.

"All that hanging around," Martin added.

"Oh no," said Ludmila. "It is good to go in the bed early. Then I can wake up morning. When I was in the Schweiz..."

David and Sheila looked puzzled.

"She means Switzerland," Martin explained. He was studying German.

"When I was in the Schweiz on the farm," continued Ludmila undeterred. "We always get up very early. Yes. Immediately after the cock."

Martin swallowed a larger amount of soup than was advisable and choked involuntarily.

"Stop it!" Sheila said to him, anticipating shock converting itself into unconfined mirth.

Ludmila appeared confused. Should she not go on with her story? There was a brief pause before she continued. Martin for some reason was biting his hand.

"When I am in the Slovakia, I have Verdauungspause from the Schweiz."

"She's saying something about indigestion," translated Martin, seeing further blank looks on both their faces.

"But she's only had soup," protested Sheila.

Ludmila was getting up. "So, hello. Nice to meet you." She was smiling at Martin. "And bringing bicycle. It is nice tradition."

"Good night!" they all said.

The next morning arrived bright and sunny.

"Did you sleep well?" Martin asked her.

Ludmila was already up and searching for a packet of muesli. Disdainfully, she returned the Coco Pops to the cupboard.

"Too sweety," she said. "Who is eating this? It is for children."

"Well, I do sometimes," Martin replied, suddenly self-conscious.

"It's okay," she said, dismissively. "You are young enough."

"Nearly sixteen," he said a touch defensively.

"I don't criticise the Coco Pops," she said. "But muesli is much better. Have you tried?"

Martin shook his head.

"When I was in the Sweaterland, we eat all the time. Much more than in the Slovakia."

"Switzerland," corrected Martin.

"Yes," said Ludmila, emptying half a packet of Grape Nuts into a bowl. "And who is eating this? The grandfather, I suppose?"

"Ludmila," Martin began. "He isn't my grandfather. He's my *father*. I know he's a bit of an old fart but..."

Ludmila put down her spoon slowly.

"Oh, I'm so sorry," she said. "I have made big mistake. I just thought..."

"No, no. It's okay. Well, it's just I happen to be the youngest."

"I see. So there are more of you?"

"Well, yes. Divided into brothers, really."

"How many?" she asked.

"Five," said Martin.

"Oh, it's very big!" Ludmila exclaimed. "You must be Catholic."

"They converted," said Martin. "I think mum had a crush on a priest at the time, or so they tell me. It was a week after the wedding."

"Is it good?" Ludmila asked.

Martin wasn't sure. "It depends which way you look at it."

"I would like to see your brothers," she announced. "Do you have photo?"

Martin had to think for a second. There was probably one from Joe's wedding. He fetched it down from above the fridge.

"Six," muttered Ludmila. "Is good. And this one?" She pointed to the photograph of a sibling in a kilt. "Has very nice knees. Is very handsome."

"Ben," confirmed Martin. "He's away at college."

"Is very tall. Very big. Ben, you say?"

"Yes."

"Big Ben," she giggled. "And this one is also nice."

"Matthew," said Martin.

"He has good eyes. Nice..."

"He's living in London."

"Škoda," said Ludmila, with a 'sh'. "Big škoda! What a putty!"

"I think you mean 'pity'," said Martin.

"Pity. Yes. Pity for me. I like your brothers too much."

There was a moment's silence.

"And now I will have to say sorry," Ludmila reflected.

"Why?" Martin asked. "You've done nothing wrong."

"No. To your father," she said. "I call him grandfather. It is a little rude."

"He won't have noticed. He doesn't listen half the time. He'll take grandfather as a compliment. As a mark of respect." He tried to suppress a sly smirk which would have given way to a giggle.

"And another thing?" Ludmila asked, polishing off the cereal.

"Yes," said Martin.

"What is old fart?"

The following afternoon, after having done some of her initial chores, Ludmila asked to be shown round the farm.

"It's quite muddy," Martin said. "Have you got any boots?"

"Of course," she replied.

He could hear heavy footsteps on the floor above after she had run back to her room.

"I can always help," she offered after they had left Winston the pony who was in the middle of a sulk.

They crossed over the yard to inspect the dairy herd.

"The folks do it mainly between them and then there's Ray who helps out too."

"Even so," said Ludmila. "I have experience from the Sweaty farm."

"Swiss." Martin corrected her.

"Ah, English is too complicated," Ludmila complained. "Why do they change these names?"

They pushed open the door of the cowshed. An indignant moo greeted them.

"Oh, yoi!" Ludmila exclaimed, looking at the incumbent of the first pen. "This cow. She is beautiful! Gold and brown!"

"Jersey," he said.

Ludmila looked puzzled.

"It's a Jersey cow. Very rich milk."

She thought for a moment.

"Oh, Jersey. Yes, I see. And what is Jersey's name?"

He glanced above. "Er, that's number five, I think."

Ludmila was shocked. "They have *numbers*, not names?" she gasped.

"Well, yes."

"What! Impossible! No name? Why?"

"I don't know. They never got round to it."

"In my last country, every cow had name. It is better so. You can call them. You cannot shout 'Number five'." She thought for a moment. "What is usual name for this type of animal?"

"Well," said Martin. "There's Daisy. Ermintrude, too, I suppose."

"Er-min-trude." Ludmila was enraptured. "Er-min-trude. It is heavenly...and beautiful!"

She gazed at the eight inquiring faces that stared back at her. "I shall give names to all. It is good idea. Maybe your grandfather has problem with memory or something but I shall name every one. Not number."

She walked the length of the byre nodding to each one in turn. It was rather like a royal visit, Martin thought.

"Do you have pig, Martin, as well?" she asked.

He nodded.

"And pig has name?"

"Of course. There's Poppy and Floppy. Henbane and..."

"You see! Pig has name but not cow. It is not logical. All must have name. It is more fair. More democratic."

"Fine," said Martin. It was hard to dispute Ludmila's logic. "You go ahead."

Two weeks later Ludmila's arms were submerged in a bowl of soap suds.

"I don't know how you can get up so early," said Martin as he arrived bleary-eyed for breakfast.

"Don't you remember?" said Ludmila. "In Switterland we all get up immediately after the..."

"Yes, thank you, Ludmila," Sheila interrupted, not wishing her to complete the sentence. "I'm sure Martin remembers very well what you said before."

"But it's true," insisted Ludmila. "And anyway, you are young. You should get up early. It is best time of day."

"I'm afraid mornings are an unknown quantity as far as Martin is concerned." Sheila continued.

"That's not true!" he protested. "I'm up now, aren't I?"

At that moment the phone chose to intervene. They could hear David speaking outside in the hall. He entered looking slightly preoccupied.

"That was Ray," he said. "He's had a bit of an accident. He's managed to fall off a ladder and turn his foot over."

"Pissed, more likely," said Martin.

They all looked at him. He fell silent.

"The upshot is he's going to be off for a couple of weeks. He won't be able to walk on it."

"We could try Cyril in the village," Sheila suggested.

"Not a good idea," David replied. "Highly unreliable."

"Then look no further," announced Ludmila.

They were all taken aback at her poetic and dramatic turn of phrase.

"I can do it."

"*You* can?" said David.

"I work on the farm before and I do cows every day. It is much better than washing dishes. You should buy dishwasher."

"It's a bit of a specialist job," David continued.

"I know. Special, yes. *I* can do it."

"It's worth a try," said Sheila. "And it'd save you getting anyone in."

The next morning Ludmila was up with the lark and contentedly ensconced in the cowshed.

"There is a machine, you know," said Martin when he went in later. "It'd save you time."

"I don't bother," said Ludmila, squeezing away. "It is much better. Always nice to be hands on."

"As you like," he replied.

Ludmila's English seemed to be getting better.

"Why don't you play music to these animals?" she asked.

"Music?"

"Yes. Music is very good."

"We've never done it."

"All animals like music. My cousin had a hamster once. It liked Bartok."

"It's never been considered," Martin said.

"Why are English so unadventurous?" she complained.

Unadventurous! Martin was again impressed. He would be hard pushed to muster an equivalent in German.

"It is no matter," Ludmila said. "I shall have to sing to them."

"Feel free," replied Martin.

At various times in the early morning, a high-pitched wail could be heard coming from the milking parlour.

"Is she all right?" David asked. He was quite concerned.

"She's singing," Martin replied.

"Is that what it is? I thought she might have been stung by a wasp."

"No wasp would dare," said Martin.

For the next four weeks, Ludmila sang and milked away. Ray had still not returned.

"Do you think he *wants* to come back?" said Sheila one evening.

"I don't know," replied David. "Perhaps it's more serious than he imagined. Anyway, I'm not complaining. The yield's gone up."

"Good for Ludmila, then," said Sheila.

Thereafter, the yield for each successive month increased.

"You've got the magic touch, Ludmila," said David admiringly.

"Not magic. It's just my singing. Rosie likes it especially."

"Rosie?"

Ludmila pointed to the cow on her right with luxuriantly long eyelashes.

"Every cow has name. I said to Martin, I give name not number."

"I suppose you're right," admitted David.

"I sing Rosie's favourite song to you."

Ludmila launched immediately into an emotional ballad. After a minute or so, David performed a diplomatic exit. The higher notes struck an uncomfortable resonance with his root canal fillings.

"Very nice, Ludmila," he called from the entrance, gently fondling his jaw.

"Thanks," said Ludmila. "It's a pleasure."

It was just before Christmas that Ludmila announced she had to go home for three weeks.

"I expect you'll want to see your family," said Sheila.

"Oh no," said Ludmila. "There is important festival in our village where we kill a pig. I always go. I come back on tenth January. It's okay?"

"Well, we'll miss your milking skills but I'm sure we can cover it," said David. "You have a good break."

"Thank you," said Ludmila.

It was noticeable, in her absence that the milk yield dipped a little. Martin even went round to reassure each cow that the milkmaid *was* coming back and waved a large cardboard ten in front of them. As agreed, Ludmila arrived back early on the specified day.

"Did you have a good time?" they asked.

"Not bad," she said. "But this year, pig not so good."

"And your family, are they well?" Sheila asked.

"Thank you," said Ludmila. She took out a bottle of plum brandy. "This is for you. For special occasion."

"Like my birthday on Friday, perhaps?" said Martin.

David examined the alcohol content of the bottle. "I think maybe not," he said. "It's one glass of wine for you or nothing."

"Parents," said Martin afterwards. "It's so embarrassing."

On the Friday evening a pervasive smell of cabbage soup and roast pork filled the kitchen.

"It is Slovak meal," said Ludmila. "I cook for Martin."

"Cheers!" they said.

"Na Zdravie!" said Ludmila. "Here's to nice future!"

Sheila began to clear away the soup bowls.

"It means I'm legal now," said Martin. "Sixteen!"

There was a brief silence.

"Legal for what?" enquired Ludmila.

Ludmila's return was greeted with enthusiasm in the dairy. A loud mooing marked her arrival to the milking stool. The temporary blip in the yield became a surge by March.

"I don't know how she does it," said David. "There must be a special knack."

"Yes, you do," said Martin. "You were there when she sang to them. They really like it."

"Yes, I was, wasn't I?" replied David, recalling the experience only too well.

At the end of September a letter from the Tatras came, followed by another from Zurich.

"Is everything okay, Ludmila?" Sheila asked, noticing a preoccupied look on Ludmila's face.

"It is my aunty," came the reply. "Her kitchen blow up in gas explosion. I never trust that cooker. Always strange noise in oven."

"I see," said Sheila. "Will you need some time to go back?"

"Of course. I must go to help my aunty. But maybe only one or two weeks and I think kitchen is fine. No, the other letter is from Switzerland. They want me to return to farm there."

"I see," said Sheila. "Yes, well, you've been a great help here. We shall miss you."

"And I shall miss cows," replied Ludmila tearfully.

On Ludmila's final evening, Martin was helping her with her packing.

"So many presents," said Ludmila. "It is very kind." She looked at one of the packets to go in her suitcase. "I have never had apricots before."

"There's a first time for everything," said Martin.

"Yes," said Ludmila, gazing at him.

"So after your aunty, it's back to Switzerland?"

She nodded. "They ask me back. Write very long letter."

"We'll miss you," he said. "*I* will, too."

She drew nearer to him.

"And I shall miss *you*," she said. There was a pause. "It's great pity you live with your parents."

"I suppose they have to live somewhere."

She was pressing down a second packet of prunes.

"Also shame I didn't meet your brothers."

"They were here when you were away."
"Ben and Matthew?"
"All of them. It was Christmas."
"Ah, yes. Pity," she repeated.
"Oh well, you'll be getting up early in Switzerland. All those chickens. Early risers," he laughed.

Ludmila looked puzzled. "No," she said. "There were no chickens on Switzerland farm. Not one."

"But I thought... You said... Early mornings? After the ..."
She laughed and closed the suitcase. "No. Not one."
Martin suddenly felt himself blushing.
In her hand was a small rectangular object.
"I make tape," she said "Special. It is for cows."
She kissed him softly on the cheek.